Claudia's Five-Dollar Horse

by
NATLEE KENOYER

Illustrated by Everett Raymond Kinstler

DUELL, SLOAN AND PEARCE
New York

CONTENTS

1. THE LETTER

DENNY and Claudia jumped to their feet as their mother came hurrying up the driveway waving a letter in her hand.

"From your Dad," she called. It was late in May and the day was pleasant and warm. "From Camp Evans. Oh, I hope it's good news." Denny folded his Scout knife, carefully wiping off the bits of dirt that still clung to the wide blade. It was the blade he used when he played mumblety-peg. He pushed the knife deep in his pocket and then pulled the jeans firmly on his slim hips. After quickly shoving a stray lock of sandy hair from his forehead, he yanked a lawn chair in place for his mother.

"Let me open it, Mom," Claudia begged, reaching for the envelope.

"Sit down and we'll see what Daddy has to say." Mary Wolff tore a corner from the envelope and then slipped her finger along the fold making a neat tear. "I hope he got his promotion." There was a worried frown across her forehead, and her glance brushed each youngster as she pulled the folded sheet of paper from the envelope and began to read silently.

Denny studied his mother's smooth face. There were slight streaks of gray in the hair that had once been as

3

brown as Claudia's. Claudia switched her pony tail and sighed.

"What does he say, Mom?" Denny was impatient.

"Maybe he's going to get another leave," Claudia suggested. "Maybe they'll give him a leave with his promotion."

"Fat chance," Denny sniffed. "He only gets one leave a year."

Their mother put the letter down and looked from one expectant face to the other. "Children," she began, "we're in trouble."

"Is Dad all right?" Denny leaned forward, and Claudia sat down hard.

"Your father is all right ... it's the ranch." Their mother took a deep breath. "We can't keep the ranch." Denny straightened up, walked to the edge of the lawn, and shoved his hands deep in his pockets.

"Why can't we keep the ranch?" Claudia spoke sharply. "We've already got it. We've got a horse and a stable, and we're living here."

"I know, dear." Her mother smoothed a strand of stray hair from Claudia's forehead. "You see, your father was expecting a promotion, and we knew we could handle the ranch if it went through." She sighed. "We were so sure."

"Couldn't we borrow some money somewhere?" Claudia cried. "We can't give up the ranch."

Denny walked back to face them. "Maybe I can earn more," he said quietly. "We've made enough to buy Blaze and keep him."

"I know, but this is so much more than that," his

4

mother reminded him. "And you still have to take care of Blaze."

"Why can't we make money off the ranch?" Claudia insisted. "That's what ranches are for."

"We thought the prune crop might take us along until the promotion came through ... but there was only enough to pay the taxes." She hesitated. "We can only pay the interest for the next two months. We can't go on after that. We'll have to put the ranch up for sale to get our equity out of it."

"But Blaze," Denny said. "What about Blaze? Will we have to give him up?"

Their mother shrugged her shoulders with resignation. "We'll see about him." She squeezed Denny's arm. "I don't want to make any promises—we'll see what we can do."

"Last summer was the best we've ever had." Claudia wiped at her eyes. "When I think of all the lawns you cut to save for Blaze."

"And the baby sitting you did," Denny broke in. He looked toward the stable where the red chestnut stood looking at them over the rail fence, flicking the flies from his flanks with a lazy tail. The large pepper tree threw its flickering shade over the stable and part of the lawn that separated the paddock from the house.

"It took a whole year to save ninety dollars." Claudia sighed. "I guess it would take a lot more than that to pay for this place." She whirled to Denny. "We just can't give Blaze up."

"It would be awful," Denny said grimly. "After Uncle Tom teaching us to ride and everything."

5

"At least you have a trophy to show that your year wasn't wasted," their mother said. "On top of that you've had a whole wonderful summer with Blaze."

"And I've just lived all winter waiting for summer vacation again," Claudia murmured. "Why did we have to wait so long to find out that we can't keep the ranch?"

"We didn't know," their mother explained. "We were so sure the promotion would come and your father would be a major by this time. We've saved so long. We thought we had enough to tide us over until your father got his new rank."

"But why isn't Daddy going to be a major?" Claudia asked.

"Who knows why?" Denny muttered. "Well, I guess we can forget about shows for this year."

"And why so?" Claudia's eyes were bright. "We can still be in another show. We don't have to move right away."

For a moment there was a hopeful glint in Denny's eyes. "It wouldn't be any good," he said finally. "Just about the time we were ready to go to a show something would happen." Their mother shook her head sadly and went into the house.

Denny walked over and leaned against the pepper tree. Claudia grinned as she followed him. "Why don't we try ... what have we got to lose?" Then she clapped her hand over her mouth.

"Don't remind me," Denny said. He looked up the driveway. The spring flowers were beginning to poke their buds through the spokes of the wagon wheels on each side of the gate posts. The sign showed a W with small wings

6

on each side. Denny and Claudia had spent one rainy
Sunday planning the sign, and Uncle Tom had helped
paint it in neat block letters that read: The Flying W
Ranch—J. T. Wolff. "It looks like a real ranch," Denny
muttered.

"It is a real ranch," Claudia spoke up. "It's good for
something, and I wish we could figure it out." She half
closed her eyes.

The acre of fenced pasture was a bright green. The nine
acres of prunes began at the north side of the property
and made an ell around back to the east where they came
to the pasture fence. The low-roofed ranch house sprawled
on a slight knoll that looked toward the driveway.

The one-stall stable was barn-red like the house. The
eucalyptus rails enclosing the pasture gave the place a
rustic look as they continued across the front of the ranch.

"Uncle Tom was going to take me into Lost Hills Canyon this summer," Claudia mused. "If I'd had a horse of
my own I could have gone last summer with you."

"You could have rented one," Denny said.

"Not me," Claudia said. "I'm only going to spend the
money I earn on Blaze or a horse of my own."

"It sure was fun," Denny said. "I guess we followed
all the trails that lead to the creek. I was hoping to meet
some kids my own age with horses—you know, and trail
with them. Maybe even form a Trail Club." His smile
faded. "No use to plan now."

"I'd plan anyway," Claudia said. "I'd have fun as long
as possible." She jerked her head and the pony tail
swished back and forth. "You can always have fun with
me."

7

"Yes, but you're my sister and you're only twelve," Denny said.

"Yes, and don't forget I own half of Blaze," Claudia said. "And I won't sell my half, no matter what. I'll keep him if we have to move into a tent ... unless I get another horse."

"No chance of that now," Denny said. "If we get to keep Blaze we'll be lucky." He kicked a stone angrily. "We don't even know that yet."

"Wouldn't it be wonderful if someone with a million dollars came along and gave us all the money we need?" Claudia said dreamily.

"Don't be silly," Denny scoffed. "That only happens in the movies. Any time we want anything we have to work for it."

"O.K. then," Claudia said quickly. "Let's work for the ranch." She paused. "Uncle Tom will know what to do."

"Well, he knows all about horses but he can't do anything about the ranch," Denny announced. "He only gets a pension."

Even as they talked a pickup truck turned into the driveway and parked near the stable. A slim, elderly man with a white mustache climbed out. Shoving the Western hat to the back of his head, he smiled at them and reached into his shirt pocket for a pipe and a can of tobacco.

"Well, kids, I thought you'd be out riding," he said.

"Hi, Uncle Tom." Denny pushed his slim fourteen-year-old length away from the tree. He looked at Uncle Tom with an unsmiling face. Claudia poked at the ground with the toe of her shoe.

Uncle Tom stopped, held the lighted match until it

8

curled its burned end and then went out. He took the unlit pipe from his mouth. "Well, well." His smile faded. He pulled at his mustache, chuckled, and lit another match. "I was just down to Kendall's stables. They're planning some good trail rides this spring if Sam Kendall can find a steady trail boss. Maybe we can join them." He looked from one to the other, pulling on his pipe with long, fitful puffs. Denny didn't answer, but shoved his hands deep into the pockets of his jeans and looked off toward the pasture.

"Well, Denny, he has to know." Claudia pulled at Denny's shirt.

"What's happening around here?" Uncle Tom was perplexed. He puffed thoughtfully. "I've never seen you two like this. Is Blaze all right?" The red chestnut still stood with his head over the top rail of the corral.

Their mother came quietly out of the house. Her expression was sober and she still had the letter in her hand. She smiled faintly at Uncle Tom as she greeted him and handed him the letter. Uncle Tom took the letter, held it a moment as he scanned the three pairs of brooding eyes. Claudia pulled her pony tail around and began chewing the ends until her mother pulled it away. Denny opened his Scout knife and whittled thin slivers off the bark of the pepper tree. Uncle Tom unfolded the letter. A moment later he put it down and knocked the ashes from his pipe.

"I wish there was something we could do," their mother said. "It's so terrible for the children. After living on Army posts for so many years we just couldn't wait for them to have a place of their own."

"Well, now, let's not worry in haste," Uncle Tom said. "Maybe, if you cut down on the orchard care ... ?"

"I don't think it would help much," Mary explained. "It has to be disked and sprayed and the dead wood cut out every year." She hesitated. "There just isn't anything you can leave undone."

"Now, Mary," Uncle Tom said, "you're not being driven off the old homestead today."

"Don't joke, Tom," their mother protested.

"You know I don't joke about things like this," Uncle Tom said. "Anything that concerns you folks concerns me too." He lit his pipe again. "If there is anything I can do you've only to ask. I wish I had more than a small pension to offer."

"You're a wonderful friend, Tom," their mother assured him. "I don't know what Jim and I would have done without you, and the children, too." She smoothed her dress and straightened her apron around her slim hips. "I guess we should have waited until we knew about the promotion, but this place was for sale and we were afraid it would be sold to someone else if we waited." She clasped her hands together. "I've even thought of going to work but I'm not trained for anything. Claudia is too young to leave at home without supervision. I wouldn't put that responsibility on Denny." She sighed and brushed a hand across her forehead. "If we could just make half the payment somehow, it might work." They were all silent with thought. The warm sun and the quiet surrounded them.

Blaze neighed and Blue, the Australian sheep dog, walked out of Blaze's stall and slumped drowsily against the water trough. A field mouse scurried across the corral and skidded through the door into the stall.

"Look!" Claudia pointed. "And Blue didn't even see it."

"Remember the night we found Blue in Blaze's stall?" Denny grinned. Their mother shook her head and wiped a tear from the corner of her eye. Uncle Tom clumsily patted her shoulder.

Claudia and Denny wandered over to the fence and stood smoothing Blaze's ear. Blaze leaned hard against their hands and closed his eyes as he enjoyed the scratching. Their mother followed and reached to smooth Blaze's muzzle. "Why don't you children go for a ride?" she said. "The grocery list and five dollars are on the table. Would you and Denny ride to the store and bring back a few things?"

Denny brought Blaze out of the stall. Claudia got the grooming tools and they brushed him until the red coat glistened. Frequently Claudia stopped to put her arms around Blaze's neck and lay her cheek against his nose. Denny placed the saddle on the smooth back and cinched it firmly. He tied a lead rope to the saddle, climbed on, and then helped Claudia to a position behind the cantle. Claudia hooked her fingers through the belt loops of Denny's jeans.

"I guess we'll be right back," Denny said.

"Why don't you stop at Kendall's while you're down there," Uncle Tom suggested.

"Why bother?" Denny growled, half to himself. "No use meeting any new kids."

11

"Well, I think it would be swell," Claudia said brightly and bounced her heels against Blaze's flank.

Denny urged Blaze into an easy flat walk as they left the lane and turned onto the road. Uncle Tom and their mother watched them go. They rode in silence for some minutes.

"I wonder ..." Denny mused.

"What?" Claudia asked.

"I wonder just how long we can live on the ranch," he said.

"Why, forever," Claudia breathed against his back.

2. THE MARE

BLAZE trotted quietly along the soft shoulder of the road.

"Sometimes I wish we'd never bought Blaze," Denny muttered.

Claudia squeezed him tightly around the waist and spoke sharply, "Don't say that, Denny."

"Well, if we didn't have him there wouldn't be a chance of losing him," Denny said angrily.

"No matter what happens we won't have to give him up, Denny, and we won't lose the ranch either." Claudia was confident.

"What do you mean?" Denny pulled Blaze up sharply and half turned in the saddle.

"Oh, we'll figure something out," Claudia assured him. "Uncle Tom will know and besides we haven't even tried yet." She thought a moment. "Let's ask Kendall's for work."

"I thought you knew something for sure," Denny scoffed as he urged Blaze forward again. "They'd never hire us."

"We know how to clean stalls and feed horses," Claudia went on. "You could take people on trail rides into Lost Hills Canyon."

"They'd never let me do that," Denny said. "A guy has to be sixteen before anyone will hire him for a real job."

"Uncle Tom took you clear to the bottom of the canyon by the creek, didn't he?" Claudia insisted. "All you have to do is go down and come back up again."

"Yeah, but people who don't know the trails could get lost." Denny sat back in the saddle. "Uncle Tom said no one should go in there without a guide. I could find my way in and out all right."

"Well, then, it's all solved." Claudia started to hum.

"It isn't solved," Denny said. "It's just an idea you've got."

"Well, it's a good idea," Claudia said. "I have some others too. We could board horses ... and we could train 'em."

13

Denny was thoughtful. "We do have some lumber left. We could build a lean-to for Blaze and rent his stall. But—" He shrugged. "We haven't enough lumber to finish it."

"Sure, that way Blaze can help too. He'd want to so he could live with us forever," Claudia agreed.

"That would mean more hay, though." Denny frowned.

"Well, we could build two stalls and have two boarders."

"Yeah, but where are we going to get the money?" Denny put in. "Every time you turn around it costs money. Besides, we don't have even one boarder yet and I don't know where to look for one. You're always getting me worked up."

"We'll get some from Mr. Kendall," Claudia said brightly.

"Huh! He's not going to let you have one of his boarders," Denny growled. "That's how he makes money."

"Well, suppose he gets too many and hasn't room for any more," Claudia said.

"You're dreaming," Denny snapped.

They came down the hill toward the stables where a large sign made an arch over the lane, Kendall's Riding Academy. The long green barns stretched in a C-shape with a riding ring in the center. They could see horses being worked in the ring and along the tie-rack other horses were being groomed and saddled. The door of the tack room stood open and long lines of saddles on racks could be seen inside. Nearby a blacksmith was pounding a hot shoe on an anvil.

The small, flat valley was dry and the last green spring

grass was turning yellow. The oblong pasture back of the barn that ended at the river was alive with a mirage of rainbows as the sprinkler system lazily swept its spray over the hungry grass. To the west lay the quarry that formed the barrier to Lost Hills Canyon. The Kendall stables nestled at the base of the hills with their long sheds pointing like arrows toward the mountains. Claudia sighed. Denny grinned at the wistful expression on her face and sat looking down at the busy scene.

"I'd love to work there," Claudia said. "Look at all those horses." She leaned around Denny until she almost lost her balance. Denny pulled her back and she made a face at him. They rode down the sloping lane to one of the hitching rails and stopped. A heavy-set, bushy-haired man with bulging arm muscles was examining the legs of a bay horse. He picked up each foot and moved the animal about without effort. He looked up and nodded. Denny climbed down and handed the reins to Claudia.

"How do you do, sir." Denny put on his best manner. "I would like to ask about work."

The man put the horse's foot down and straightened up. "I don't need any help. I've always got a bunch of kids hanging around here trying to earn enough for rides. Most of them don't know one end of a horse from the other."

"We have our own horse," Claudia put in. "And we take care of it too."

"Oh, you too?" The man grinned up at her.

"No," Claudia said simply. "It's for my brother." She went on quickly. "He knows all the trails in Lost Hills Canyon."

15

"You do?" The man's eyes flicked with interest.
"Well!" He rubbed a large hand across his chin. "I'm
Sam Kendall." He looked closely at Denny. "I have a
trail boss ... that is ... when he's able. He doesn't know
much about Lost Hills Canyon ... and neither do I. Don't

EVERETT RAYMOND KINSTLER

have time to wander around the country. But I don't need any amateurs!''

"Denny has been clear to the bottom by the creek," Claudia explained. "He never gets lost in the canyon."

"Is that so?" Kendall replied. "You're pretty young." He moved back to the horse again.

Claudia climbed down and loosened the tie-rope. Denny snapped it around Blaze's neck and tied him to the hitch rack.

"Well, it's a good thing you found my brother." Claudia smiled at Sam Kendall. "Any time you need a good trail boss you'll know where to get one."

"You're a busy little thing." Kendall reached over

and chucked her under the chin. "Do you always go around blowing your brother's horn?"

"Well," Claudia told him, "he can do almost anything." She gave Denny a sideways look. "And besides we need the ..." She clapped her hand to her mouth as Denny placed a well-balanced foot on her toe.

"She just does that to keep on the good side of me," Denny finished lamely.

"Your stables are real nice," Claudia said.

"Would you like to see them?" Mr. Kendall chuckled.

"Yes, sir!" Denny pushed Claudia behind him. "I sure would." He leaned against Claudia as Mr. Kendall turned toward the shed row. "Stay here ... you want to spoil everything."

Denny followed after Sam Kendall. Claudia lagged behind and then turned around and walked in the other direction. She went along looking over the half doors into each stall. A rickety truck rambled down the hill with an unpainted horse trailer bumping along behind it. Claudia paused in her inspection, glanced after the retreating backs of Denny and Sam Kendall, then turned to watch the truck.

It came to a sliding, dusty stop and a small, thin, unkempt man stepped out. He ran a dirty hand across his sweaty forehead as he shoved his hat back. He looked around expectantly and then gave Claudia an angry glance.

"Where's the boss around here?" He glanced toward Sam Kendall and Denny as they came out of a stall and closed the door. "You the boss?" he called.

Sam Kendall locked the catch on the door, said something to Denny, and came back. He looked the man over. "Well?" he snapped.

"I got a horse I wanta sell." The man unscrewed the bolt of the tail gate and let it down with a bang. Claudia gasped and Denny edged closer as they stood looking at the small bay mare standing in the trailer. She was bony thin. Her hips stood out like wings and her backbone displayed every vertebra as she slumped with her head down. The man backed her out and she stood looking like a skeleton covered with dull, brown hair.

"Oh, the poor thing!" Claudia ran to the mare's head and stroked the thin face. The mare nuzzled her hand and then reached up and slowly sniffed her face. "She likes me!" Claudia hugged the thin neck and smiled at Denny.

"She looks starved to me." Sam Kendall's face flushed angrily. "Is this your horse?"

"She belonged to my nephew," the man said. "He went into the Navy and left her with me. I can't afford to feed her so I'm selling her."

"Did she look like this when he left her with you?" Sam Kendall asked.

"Naw," the man grunted. "He had some big-fangled idea about her but I ain't got no money to waste on feed for a horse." He looked around. "I'll sell her for fifty dollars."

"The way she looks right now she isn't worth a plugged nickel." Sam Kendall showed his anger. "I ought to report you to the S.P.C.A."

"Isn't that the Humane Society?" Denny asked.

"Yes," Mr. Kendall said. "That animal should be taken away from him."

"I gotta get my money outa this horse." The man ignored Mr. Kendall and glanced around. "I'll take less."

"No one is going to buy that horse in the condition she's in," Sam Kendall snapped. "Take it home and feed it."

"All right, make me an offer." The man glared at them all. "I can't go buying any feed."

"I wouldn't buy the horse in the first place," Sam Kendall said. "And if I did I wouldn't give you five dollars for her." He took Denny by the arm. "Come on, son, I've got no time for a man like that."

The man ran after Kendall and grabbed his arm. "I'll take it."

Sam Kendall jerked out of his reach. "Go on, get lost, before I report you." When Mr. Kendall and Denny walked away everyone else went back to their horses or began talking in groups. Claudia still stood with her arms around the mare's neck.

The man stood looking after Mr. Kendall. He turned slowly and came back to the little mare. He jerked her roughly out of Claudia's grasp and started to lead her up the ramp into the trailer.

"Would you sell her to me for five dollars?" Claudia followed him up the ramp. The man stopped, turned to look at her. He stood for a long minute, twisting the lead rope nervously in his hands. He glanced over her head in the direction that Sam Kendall and Denny had taken and then quickly around the stableyard. "I have the five dollars." Claudia waited.

"You can't come back for your money," he warned. He

led the mare back down the ramp. "O.K., little girl, you've got yourself a deal."

Claudia plunged her hand deep into her jean pocket and brought forth the five dollars wrapped in the grocery list. She unfolded it slowly and handed it to him. "I'd like a receipt, please."

The man scowled, dug a stubby pencil from his shirt pocket, hesitated, and then took the grocery list from her hand. "I ain't takin' her back ... for no reason." He read the grocery list and then turned it over and smoothed out the paper. He wrote quickly, thrust it into her hand, and hurriedly pushed the tail gate into place. Jumping into the truck, he gunned the motor until the fenders shook and then he roared out of the stableyard.

Claudia stood with the receipt in her hand and then put a hand on the little mare's nose. Suddenly she let her breath out with a gasp. Her face paled and she held tightly to the lead rope. A tear rolled down her cheek and she snuffed hard. When Denny came back she was leaning against the rough brown coat.

"What's the matter, Claudia, where's the man who owns this horse?" Denny's face showed concern and he glanced at the bare courtyard.

"He's gone," Claudia cried. "I bought her with the grocery money."

"You what?" Denny's mouth dropped open and he walked around the mare shaking his head. "Boy, are you gonna get it!"

"I couldn't help it," Claudia cried. "She's so little. And that man was mean to her, I know he was."

"You'd better get him back here fast," Denny warned.

"I don't know his name or where he lives," Claudia said. Sam Kendall came around the corner and stopped short when he saw the mare.

"She bought it," Denny said.

"Oh, no!" Mr. Kendall chuckled. "What do you think you're going to do with that crowbait?"

"She's not crowbait and I'm going to keep her and fatten her up and love her!" Claudia was defiant.

"We can't keep her," Denny insisted. "Do you know where that man lives? We have to get the money back."

"I never saw him before," Sam Kendall said. He ran a hand over the thin back. "She's got some breeding. Wouldn't look bad if she was filled out."

"The man said he wouldn't take her back," Claudia said. "I'm glad I don't know his name or where he lives."

"Didn't you get a receipt?" Sam Kendall gave her a severe glance.

"Sure." Claudia held it out.

"The nearest I can make out of this scribble is Bill Binder." Sam Kendall studied the signature. "That must be his name but that doesn't tell much. I don't know where he lives."

"Mom isn't going to like this," Denny said. "You know we can't have another horse."

"Mom will love her, too," Claudia said.

"All right, get on," Denny snapped. "Ride her home and just see what happens."

Claudia's eyes widened and she gave Denny a surprised look. "I wouldn't ride her now. She's much too thin. We'll lead her behind Blaze."

22

"Hope you don't get into trouble over this," Mr. Kendall said. "Sometimes, having a big heart isn't the best thing."

"Well," Denny said, "it sure isn't right now."

"Everything will be all right," Claudia said. "When you do something good it has to be."

3. CRICKET

WHEN Claudia and Denny rode into the yard their mother and Uncle Tom came out of the house to meet them. The youngsters saw the looks of puzzlement and consternation on their faces and Denny poked his elbow in Claudia's side as she gave him an uneasy glance.

"Brace yourself," Denny warned under his breath. Claudia stiffened her shoulders and almost dropped the lead rope. Blue ran from the stable and sniffed at the mare's heels.

"Claudia," her mother spoke sharply, "where did you get that?" Uncle Tom walked up and ran a hand down the bony backbone. He stepped back and squinted, turning his head from side to side. He raised his eyebrows at

Denny and Denny returned the look with hunched shoulders.

"Well..." Claudia began. She leaned against Denny for support.

Denny sighed. "She bought it."

"Bought it!" Their mother looked from one face to the other unbelievingly. Her glance traveled over the little mare and then to Uncle Tom. An amused smile twitched the corners of his mustache. Their mother frowned at him. She turned back to the waiting children. "With what?"

"With the grocery money," Claudia said and climbed down. Mrs. Wolff stood waiting. Claudia took a step toward Uncle Tom, then another step, and slipped her hand into his. He squeezed it and she relaxed a little.

"I'd say you made a good buy," Uncle Tom commented. "Best time to buy a horse is when you can see the frame." He nodded wisely. "This one's got good conformation. I'd say she's a four-year-old." He dropped Claudia's hand and opened the mare's mouth and looked at her teeth. "She's either one of the larger breeds of ponies or a small horse." He patted Claudia on the shoulder. "I'd say you're a good horse trader."

"That's what Mr. Kendall said." Claudia's eyes probed her mother's. "He said she just needed to put on some fat."

"Tom!" their mother scolded. "Claudia!" She folded her arms across her chest. "You seem to forget we have another problem that we haven't solved. This is just more trouble. You'll have to take it back."

"She can't take it back," Denny said. "No one knows the man and no one knows where he lives."

24

"I can pay you back, Mom, honest," Claudia said seriously.

"And what do you think you're going to eat tonight?" her mother said quickly. "That was the grocery money you spent." She turned to Uncle Tom. "Imagine buying a horse for five dollars."

"Mr. Kendall wouldn't give the man five dollars for her," Denny put in.

"You never mind, Denny," Claudia began on a stern note. "I can fatten her up so she'll be the prettiest horse in the whole world ... except Blaze, of course."

"I'll give Claudia the five dollars," Uncle Tom offered.

"No, you won't," their mother said quickly. "That isn't the question. If we weren't worried about the ranch I'd say it was fine."

"It will be all right, Mom," Claudia said anxiously. "With the baby sitting I do every Saturday afternoon I can feed her for a long time." She stopped at the expression on her mother's face. "Honest, Mom, I couldn't help it. She needed me and I had to rescue her. That man was mean to her."

"Well..." Her mother hesitated.

"There, you see." Claudia smiled. "Everything will be just fine."

"You're always saying that," Denny put in. "Saying it doesn't make it so."

"I didn't say you could keep her." Her mother stood firm.

"Well," Claudia said easily, "can't I keep her until something terrible happens ... like having to move from the ranch?"

"She has a point," Uncle Tom chuckled. He gave Claudia a serious wink. "You've got a feeding job there, young lady."

"Tom!" their mother interrupted. "You're not much help."

"I guess I'm with the kids," he put in lamely.

"Claudia." Her mother put an arm across her shoulders. "Are you willing to keep this horse, become attached to it, and then give it up when the time comes?" She

shook her head sadly. "I don't think you realize what you're bringing on yourself."

"But, Mom, I won't have to give her up ... wait and see," Claudia said brightly. "Everything is turning out just right.'' She took Denny's arm. ''Now, we each have a horse!'' Denny nodded grimly.

Their mother sighed. The little mare whinnied and Claudia rubbed the bony nose and adjusted the rope around her neck.

''What are you going to do for a bridle?'' Denny fingered the rope.

''I'll show you how to make an Indian bridle,'' Uncle Tom offered.

''Will it cost anything?'' Denny asked.

''I think I have a piece of rawhide at home,'' Uncle Tom explained. ''You just run a piece over the lower jaw and put it through a loop in the rawhide and then you ride with one rein.''

''How do you guide with one rein?'' Claudia asked.

''You neck-rein like you do when you ride Western,'' Uncle Tom explained. ''You pull the rein to the right when you turn that way and lay it over his neck when you turn left.''

''That will be fine,'' Claudia said happily. ''I guess I'll have to ride bareback for a while.''

''We can take turns with the saddle,'' Denny offered. ''What are you going to name her?''

Claudia looked thoughtful. ''She's small and dark. I don't know much about her yet.'' She paused. ''Sometimes you have to know a horse for a while before you can pick a real good name.''

''Claudia!'' her mother warned.

''You name her, Mom,'' Claudia begged.

''I'm not going to have anything to do with this,'' her mother said.

27

"I ought to name her right now, though." Claudia avoided her mother's glance.

"She's skinny and her legs look long," Denny said. "How about Skinny?"

"I don't think you're nice." Claudia frowned.

"She's tiny and I'll bet she's quick," Uncle Tom said. "She looks like Cricket to me."

"That's it!" Claudia clapped her hands and jumped up and down. "That's what we'll call her, Cricket."

"I just don't know," their mother interrupted. "It seems that troubles come in bunches. I wish your father were here."

"Don't worry, Mom," Claudia assured her. "Denny is going to work for Mr. Kendall. He's going to take out the trail rides."

"Claudia," Denny exploded, "how can you say that? He didn't even ask me."

"He was interested," Claudia insisted. "Especially when I told him you knew the trails clear to the bottom by the creek."

"That's fine," Uncle Tom said.

"But he didn't say he was going to hire me," Denny said. "Claudia's so sure of things." Denny stared at her coldly. "Why do you have to say such stuff?"

"Well, let's get this little mare put away," Uncle Tom suggested. "She looks as if she could stand something to eat."

"Come on, Cricket," Claudia said briskly. "Uncle Tom, haven't we enough lumber to build a lean-to?"

"There's enough to build the framework for two stalls," Uncle Tom said. "You'll have to buy lumber to enclose them but it won't take much." He thought a moment. "You really wouldn't need walls until next winter."

"None of you seem to realize..." their mother began.

"Yeah," Denny agreed. "Don't get any ideas, Claudia."

"But I do have ideas." Claudia thrust her chin out. "You see, we can have boarders."

"That might be the answer to your problem," Uncle Tom agreed. "The paddock is large enough to take care of three horses, maybe four... and you can always let them out on pasture."

"I'm not going to stay out here and listen to anyone." Their mother turned to go. "I dread the day when this all has to be changed."

Claudia looked after her. "Oh, it's going to be changed, all right." Denny led Blaze to the fence and unsaddled him. He was silent as he put him in the stall and tossed him a leaf of hay.

"Well, let's go to work on the stall then," Claudia said. "We have to have a place for Cricket anyway."

"How are we going to get boarders?" Denny broke in. "Have you thought of that?" He waited. "And we also have to have money to build with."

"We'll take our first board money and finish the stalls." Claudia was matter of fact.

"Yes, but we haven't got a boarder," Denny insisted. "I suppose you think you're going right out and get one."

"I will." Claudia stood straight and determined. She stood thinking for a moment and then led Cricket over to the stable, opened the gate, and turned her in with Blaze.

She put a leaf of hay in a corner of the paddock and stood watching with satisfaction as the little mare munched eagerly.

"Life sure would be simple if everything turned out according to Claudia." Denny scratched his head and grinned at Uncle Tom. "She makes everything sound so simple."

"Life is simple," Uncle Tom admitted. "It's just that we make it complicated."

"Paying for Blaze wasn't simple," Denny put in. "And finding jobs to make enough money to feed him wasn't simple either."

"But you did it," Uncle Tom said.

"Yes," Denny agreed. "I can't see where trying to keep this ranch is going to be simple but if you listen to Claudia you'd think it was." He turned as Claudia came toward them. "Instead of making things simple you've added another problem by buying Cricket."

"You should be glad, Denny," Claudia said stubbornly. "Now Blaze belongs to you."

"That part would be all right." Denny kicked a stone hard with the toe of his boot. "Everything would be great if we could keep the ranch."

"We're still here, aren't we?" Claudia said.

"We just got the letter today." Denny looked at her with exasperation.

"Well, tomorrow you can say we got the letter yesterday." Claudia giggled. "Anyhow, let's think about it tomorrow." Claudia addressed herself to Uncle Tom, "Now we have to get the stalls started." Uncle Tom grinned at her straight, determined little back. "Will it take long to put the framework up?" She pulled at Denny's arm. "Come on, Denny, we've got lots of work to do if we're going into business."

4. TRAIL BOSS

THE framework of the two stalls was up and every last piece of scrap wood had been used for bracing. The sheeting was on and Uncle Tom measured it for the rolled roofing that would have to be put on before rainy weather. The mangers were in but there were no solid walls. Claudia stood back and looked at the wooden skeleton of the two stalls.

"If we should get a flood of boarders, which we won't," Denny said grimly, "we won't have another thing to build with."

"If we should get a flood of boarders we could finish these stalls," Claudia countered. "Well, at least Cricket has a roof over her head and if we should get another boarder we can put the walls on both stalls. Gee, I'll be glad when they're finished."

"I wonder if there is any other place I can get a regular job?" Denny sat down. "I wish I was older, at least sixteen."

"Then you could finish the stalls," Claudia said brightly.

"I wasn't thinking of the stalls," Denny began on a stern note. "Without the ranch we won't need stalls or horses."

"Oh, the ranch will be all right," Claudia said. "We've got other things to think about."

"Well, you see to it we have other things to think about," Denny said. "I'm glad you're not twins."

Their mother came to the back door. She looked at the new framework. "You've accomplished a lot today." She opened the door wide. "Come along, I have supper waiting." Denny pushed by and went to his room. "Wash your hands, Claudia." She took Claudia's chin. "Your face could stand some cleaning, too." Uncle Tom hung his hat on a nail on the back porch and washed his hands in the sanitary tubs beside the washing machine.

When Denny came to the table he was wearing a clean Western shirt and a string tie. He pulled a chair out for his mother and then sat down.

"You look mighty sharp." Uncle Tom grinned at him. Claudia hurried into her chair.

"He looks like a dude," Claudia said.

"I like wearing Western clothes," Denny said quickly.

"If you're going into business then you have to dress the part," Uncle Tom told them and winked at their mother.

The telephone rang and their mother went to answer it.

"Denny," she called. "Mr. Kendall says his regular man is sick and wants to know if you can take out the trail ride tomorrow."

Denny glanced quickly at Claudia and Uncle Tom. He gulped once and answered weakly, "Sure . . . sure, I'll do it."

"You see," Claudia said brightly. "I told you he'd want you." Denny looked pleased and attacked his food vigorously.

"I wish I could go tomorrow," Claudia said. She shook her head. "I have to get some fat on Cricket before I can even ride out of the yard."

"You can handle her, though," Uncle Tom told her. "You can groom her and find out what she knows." He held out his cup to be filled. Their mother gave a warning glance but he avoided looking at her. "She is pretty young."

"You'll be busy while I'm working for Mr. Kendall," Denny interrupted. "Gee, I didn't think I'd get the chance."

When Denny rode into Kendall's stableyard the next morning there were six horses saddled and Mr. Kendall was waiting for him.

"There are six riders for you today." Mr. Kendall hesitated. "You're sure you know the trail?" He waited. "I'd take the ride out myself but I've been so busy running this stable that I've never had a chance to learn the country."

"Yes, sir," Denny said. "Uncle Tom took me all over the canyon. I can find my way back all right."

"Maybe you'd better not take them into the canyon,"

Mr. Kendall said. "Just ride up to the entrance and then bring them back. That will be enough for today."

"That will be easy," Denny said.

"Freddie and Clift cleaned stalls today so they've earned a ride." Sam Kendall indicated two boys who lounged against the shed row. "I'll collect from the rest and then you can get started." Freddie straightened up and gave a wave of his hand. He pulled his jeans up over his hips and walked over to look at Blaze.

"I've sure been wanting a horse," he said. "My pop says he'll get me one when I'm fifteen if I'm still in the mood."

"I saved my own money," Denny said. "That is, my sister and I did. I won't be fifteen until next fall."

"Some people are just lucky." Clift shoved a freckled hand through his red hair and gave Denny an unsmiling glance. "Think you know where you're going?"

"Sure." Denny nodded. "I've been there."

"I could take a ride out as well as you can," Clift stated. "Maybe better, I'm older."

"You've never even been to the entrance to Lost Hills Canyon," Freddie said. "Besides, he has his own horse."

"What's so great about that?" Clift snapped. "I'd find the way. I don't know what Sam Kendall wants a kid like you for."

"Well, he asked me," Denny said. "I guess that's enough."

Sam Kendall walked up. "O.K., mount up," he ordered. "You should be back in an hour and a half." He turned to Denny. "Rest the horses at the top of the mountain and then come back."

34

"How does he know what to do?" Clift put in sarcastically.

"Anyone who has a horse of his own knows how to take care of it," Sam Kendall said. "This is your first trail ride so don't run that horse up the hill."

"Who said I was going to?" Clift retorted. He swung lazily up into the saddle and sat waiting.

"Shall I loosen the cinches when we stop to rest?" Denny asked.

"Not on such a short ride," Sam instructed. "Just check them before you start back."

"Yes, sir," Denny agreed and moved his horse to the head of the line and started the group at a good walk. Freddie rode up behind him, then came three girls and a small boy. Clift brought up the rear, keeping enough space between himself and the other riders so he wouldn't have to talk to them.

"Ol' Clift is mad." Freddie giggled. "He's been after Mr. Kendall for work but all he's got is a little stall cleaning so he can take a ride."

"I guess I'm pretty lucky," Denny said.

"Clift shows off too much," Freddie said. "But, you know, he isn't afraid to do anything."

The line of riders could be seen climbing the trail along the brow of the hill above the stable. It disappeared behind a clump of scrub oak trees that shielded the trail at the first turn. The day was warm and Blaze switched his tail as he lengthened his stride. Denny glanced back frequently to see that everyone was following closely.

Freddie urged his horse up beside Denny. "I'll bet no one has been behind that wall that hides the canyon." He

35

eyed Denny. "Mr. Kendall's trail boss says it's too steep."

"It's steep all right," Denny said. "I've been as far down as the creek . . . that's nearly to the bottom of the canyon on this side. If you're a good rider the steepness doesn't bother you."

"If we hurried we could go down the trail a ways," Freddie suggested.

"It gets rough." Denny looked up at the sheer rock with the deep split in the wall where the trail continued. "I don't think the riders we have today are good enough. Besides, Mr. Kendall said to go just to the split in the rocks. Trails are deceiving. You can get delayed before you know it. We have only an hour and a half. We'd never make it back in time."

Clift rode past the others and caught up with Denny and Freddie in time to hear his comment. "I can just clean more stalls if we're late," he said.

"That wouldn't take care of the other riders," Freddie said. "Mr. Kendall might not let us go again either."

"Are you afraid of Sam Kendall?" Clift said to Denny.

"Of course not," Denny told him. "I'd like to do a good job. This is my first trail ride for him."

"I guess if you don't do a good job he won't send you again," Clift said.

"That's possible," Denny said. "Maybe I won't anyhow. His trail boss is sick today."

"He has asthma," Freddie stated. "He's sick a lot. Mr. Kendall doesn't know any of the trails so when Pete's sick there aren't any trail rides."

"Well, I could take them out," Clift insisted.

"You don't ride well enough." Freddie grinned wickedly.

"Says you," Clift said heatedly. "It wouldn't hurt to go through the split and then I'd show you how well I can ride."

"It would take experienced riders to go into the canyon." Denny nodded toward the small boy. "He's too little."

"You're not afraid, are you?" Clift gave Denny a sharp glance.

"No." Denny eyed him. "I'm never afraid when I'm on Blaze." He urged Blaze on ahead and threw back over his shoulder, "Since I've started riding a horse I've learned to take orders."

"Well, don't get tough about it," Clift snapped. Denny pressed his lips together in a thin line and pushed on ahead. He watched Blaze's bobbing head and his eyes were thoughtful. He turned to look down the line. Freddie and Clift were walking their horses close together and were deep in conversation. The others were in single file, riding along quietly.

When they reached the split in the canyon wall Denny told everyone to dismount. They climbed down and stood looking at the huge rock that had split sometime in the long past and had spread apart to make an archway large enough for a horse and rider to ride through without touching the sides. On each side of the trail large clumps of bushes tried to push across the path. "Spread along the trail," Denny called. Clift and Freddie rode on ahead to the mouth of the split and stopped. They sat on their horses and watched Denny tie Blaze to a bush before he went to help the small boy from his horse.

Denny glanced at them for a moment and started to speak. He hesitated and then turned to help the girls. One of the girls had a rock in her boot and Denny helped her remove the boot and turned it upside down. The three young riders tried to point out part of the trail they had covered. Denny pointed out the valley below that could just be seen through the gap in the hills.

Fifteen minutes later Denny started checking cinches, tightening some, adjusting the saddles, and straightening the blankets. He brushed the dirt from his clothes. "Time to be starting back." He walked up the trail looking for Clift and Freddie. He looked down the sides of the hill into the brush. "Come on, you guys, it's time to start back," he called. He waited but got no answer. Denny turned to the others. "Wait here," he told them. "I'll go up the path and get them."

He mounted Blaze and rode up the trail. There was no sign of Freddie and Clift. He came to the split in the rock and pushed through the heavy shrub that blocked the entrance to Lost Hills Canyon. Urging Blaze down the narrow, walled path, he could see the hoofprints in the powdery dust. There was no question of Freddie and Clift having been there. Denny came out of the rocky cavern of the split and looked down upon the heavily wooded maze of the canyon. He stopped Blaze and listened. There was nothing but the quiet of the trees and the chirping of the birds. Overhead a hawk sailed lazily over the canyon. The wings were like sails, but Denny could see the bird's head sweeping the landscape below. The trail curled

38

around the mountain and was soon hidden by the heavy undergrowth of trees. He shouted for Freddie. No answer. This was Clift's idea. A way to get Denny into trouble with Sam Kendall. And it would work. Denny wiped a hand across his sweaty forehead and set his hat more firmly on his head. He sat thinking for a moment. He couldn't go ahead. He glanced back the way he had come then, shrugging his shoulders, he turned Blaze until he faced up the trail and started back along the path. There was nothing to do but take the other riders back to the stable.

When Denny came out of the rocky split he found the other four riders waiting. "We'll ride back to the stable. I think the boys have gone exploring," he said by way of explanation. He rode on ahead of the group so they wouldn't see the pale line about his mouth and the shaking of his hands on the reins. Sam Kendall was going to be angry.

He kept up a hurried pace until he was in sight of the stable. When he reached the hitching rail he climbed down and tied Blaze. After helping the four riders to dismount, he secured their horses and went to look for Sam Kendall. He found him in the first stall and he came out and locked the door.

"I see you got back all right." He smiled and looked around. "Where're Clift and Freddie?"

"They went through the split in the rocks, Mr. Kendall," Denny explained. "They left as I was tying the horses when we stopped to rest."

"Why didn't you call them back?" Sam Kendall's voice

held a note of anger. Denny squared his shoulders. "Why didn't you make them stay with you?"

"I didn't think about them leaving," Denny tried to explain. "I was checking the rest of the riders and I thought they were resting on the trail." Denny watched Sam Kendall's face. "I'm sorry, Mr. Kendall. I'll go back after them but I thought I ought to get these four back first."

"Well, at least you did one thing right," Sam Kendall snapped. "That's what I get for hiring a kid."

"Mr. Kendall, I'll get them for you, I promise." Denny stood waiting. Sam Kendall glared at him and went on unsaddling horses. Denny stood for an indecisive moment, then he went over to Blaze. He loosened the cinch and pulled the saddle off. He scrubbed Blaze's back with the rubber currycomb. Turning the blankets over, he saddled him again. He swung up and turned Blaze toward the trail.

Sam Kendall jerked around. "Where do you think you're goin'?"

"I'm going to find the boys." Denny held Blaze in check. "There're a few hours of daylight left. I've got to find them before dark."

"You stay right where you are," Sam Kendall ordered. "Two's enough to be lost. I'll call the sheriff's office and get a posse."

"I know the trails, Mr. Kendall," Denny insisted. "I'll bring them back. This is my job and I'll do it."

"I'm not trusting any more to a kid," Sam Kendall snapped. He started toward the house and the telephone. Denny watched him. He walked Blaze back and forth nervously. Suddenly he threw his weight forward in the saddle. Blaze responded with a leap, and the chestnut broke into a fast gallop toward the trail.

Denny settled his hat firmly on his head and his eyes narrowed with determination. It might be hours before a posse could be gathered. In a moment he was out of sight around the brush on the trail, galloping easily up the mountainside. What difference did it make now how angry Sam Kendall would get? He'd find the boys. He knew the canyon. He'd bring the boys back and then he would never go near the stable again. Clift could have the whole thing, stall cleaning and all. Denny slowed Blaze to a trot as he came in sight of the split.

5. CANYON TRAIL

DENNY pulled Blaze to a stop and looked back down the trail. Over the trees he could barely see the roofs of the stables. Sam Kendall must be organizing a posse. If he could only find the boys and get them back before Mr. Kendall started the search! Even that might not be enough to redeem himself with Sam, but anything was worth a try. Few ever went into the canyon and its thickly brushed valley unless an experienced guide led the way down the narrow deer trails. Uncle Tom had been definite about this. Winding between two steep ridges the creek seemed to flow from a sheer cliff. From its shattered top the water worked its way down the crevices to the creek. This rocky crag guarded the south end of the canyon and defied even the deer to leap its insurmountable walls.

The creek wandered through the rocks until its pebbled bed stopped abruptly in a narrow gulch. From here it went underground to reappear, like a spring, near the stables where it joined the river. Denny urged Blaze toward the opening. The chestnut snorted and sidestepped and then plunged ahead, shoving impatiently with his muzzle, hesitating to grab a dry leaf that still hung on the almost bare shrub just beginning to sprout new growth. Denny climbed down, stared up the trail again, then taking the reins close up by the bit, he studied the ground for returning tracks. There were none.

He dived through the brush and disappeared from sight while Blaze also melted into the gloom of the huge rock after him. Bright sunshine hit him as he found himself on the wide rocky ledge that viewed the whole canyon below. Finding the stirrup, he swung into the saddle and followed the natural trail upward as it circled this portion of the rocky wall. Suddenly it turned sharply downward, narrow, spotted with loose rocks and a sprinkling of scattered deer tracks where the ground was powdery. Overlaying these tracks Denny saw the well-marked print of a horse's hoof.

He pushed through the stubborn, weathered chaparral that hugged the edges of the trail and fought to keep their part of it. Denny bent the tough branches but they only twisted in his hand and refused to break. It was rough

riding. Here the deer leaped over where the brush refused
to yield. The trail continued and the going became easier.
Everything was quiet except for the chirping of the birds.
Denny stopped to listen.

He studied the ground. The prints still headed down.
The trail twisted unevenly but was plain to see. Denny
observed the prints closely. The edges were sharp, prov-
ing they were fresh. He compared them with the deer
tracks. The outlines of the deer tracks had crumpled toward the inside. Deer must have been along this trail the
day before. Uncle Tom had taught Denny well.

Denny tapped Blaze with his heel. He stopped frequently to listen for voices and then moved deeper into the
canyon. When he could hear the tumbling of the stream he
pulled up in a sandy clearing that formed a tiny beach
dotted with large rocks. He allowed Blaze to move to the
edge of the creek for a drink, and watched Blaze's throat
move in great rolls as he sucked the water between his lips.

"Someone's been here." Denny spoke half to himself
and to Blaze. He pointed to the scrambled hoofprints.
"Looks as if he started down." Denny slid from the saddle and squatted on his heels. "I still see only one set of
prints, though." Denny stood up, scratched his head, and
leaned against Blaze. "Looks like they separated, all
right." He went on. "Come on, boy, let's find him."

Away from the sandy edge of the creek the ground was
packed, hard as a rock. Denny viewed the surrounding
area. Up the trail he saw a cracked branch and a few
pieces of thread and a bit of cloth still clinging to the stubborn twig. Denny studied the trail. Ahead it went down
out of sight. From the direction he had come it led up and

around the canyon wall, wherever there was a foothold. Clift and Freddie should have stayed together. Suppose one of them got hurt. Uncle Tom had explained the many things that could happen.

Denny turned Blaze around, gathered the reins, and climbed into the saddle. He tensed and listened. A different sound from the rustling of the trees and the calls of the birds. There it was again—plainly. "Halloo!" came faintly from down below. Denny listened again. Once more he heard the voice. Denny shouted back and then began to pick his way carefully, stopping frequently to look for tracks. Dead branches spattered in broken bits on his legs and boots, breaking with sharp cracks and filling the air with dust—except the tough chaparral which twisted at his jeans as he went by. Blaze, always alert for food, tried to snatch bites of dry grass that grew out around the rocks along the high side of the trail. When he snorted the sprays of dust and droplets blew into the air. Denny guided Blaze's head around low-hanging branches, following the course of the creek, sometimes walking on its pebbled bottom. Blaze pawed the water and sent it splashing up over the stirrups.

It was farther to the bottom of the canyon than he had remembered. Soon the creek would start underground. Denny heard a horse neigh, and Blaze nickered in answer. He headed Blaze in the direction of the sound.

"Hey, hey up there, who is it?" It was Clift's voice.

"Denny." In a few minutes he came out on a small clearing close to the creek. Clift lolled comfortably against a rock and a smile wrinkled his freckled face. He sat up slowly, regarding Denny with an air of defiance.

"I thought someone was coming," he said. "Of course, it would be you. Too much noise for a small animal." He chuckled. "Just a big animal."

Denny ignored the remark. "What was the idea of leaving the bunch?" Denny said angrily.

"A real dull trail ride." Clift's square-jawed face grimaced and he looked Denny square in the eye. "Riding with a bunch of amateurs on an easy trail. Walk up, walk back, nothing else."

"You didn't have to go," Denny said heatedly. "You knew what it would be before you went."

"I coulda taken this ride out and everyone would have had fun," Clift said harshly. "I'd have scared those kids to death with some real stories." He laughed at the thought. "They wouldn't have forgotten this ride."

"Well, I won't forget this ride," Denny bit off the words. "Nor you. You got me into a lot of trouble." He glanced about. "Where's Freddie?"

"How do I know?" Clift stared at him coldly. "He wanted to turn back so I told him to go ahead. I decided to see what was at the bottom of this canyon." He straightened up. "What're you goin' to do about it?"

"I'm going to get you and Freddie out of here and back to the stable before Mr. Kendall brings a posse to look for you." Denny climbed down and dropped the reins to the ground.

"Oh, a posse, eh." Clift grinned, chuckled, and sat down again. "A posse, well, let 'em come. Let 'em come in and find me. I don't need you to get me outa here." He rolled to one side, brushing the dust from his jeans and then stood up again. "I'm older than you, I'll say what we'll

45

do. You can follow me, I'll lead *you* out.'' Clift untied his horse and pulled himself up into the saddle. Denny was silent. His face flushed with anger, but he bit his lip and kept quiet. This was no time to fight.

Denny picked up the reins, mounted, and followed Clift up the slope. A few minutes later Denny suddenly reined up and stopped.

Clift gave him a sideways glance. ''Well?''

''You're going the wrong way,'' Denny said.

''This is the way I came down,'' Clift argued. ''I remember that tree over there.''

''If you keep going you're going to end right back where you started,'' Denny insisted.

''I know I'm right,'' Clift yelled and jerked his horse off stride and the animal reared, swerving around on the narrow trail. ''I'll show you.'' Denny watched him as he whirled his horse again and went trotting along the path. Denny sighed with disgust and followed slowly, his brows knit in thought. A few yards farther they turned sharply toward the creek. A little distance ahead was a small gully. Clift pulled his horse to a stop and sat looking across. Across the gully was the exact place where Denny had found him a few minutes before. Denny sat waiting.

''Well,'' Clift growled, ''let's hear you say something.'' He gave his horse a hard kick in the ribs and the animal leaped over the gully. He landed stiff-legged on the other side and Clift rolled over the saddle horn, landing on his shoulder. He leaped to his feet and, grabbing the reins, whipped the horse repeatedly across the shoulders. The horse lunged in an effort to get away.

''That's enough!'' Denny yelled. ''Stop that!'' He

46

jumped Blaze easily and shook his feet free from the stirrups. He swung down. His movements were quick, reflect-
ing the boiling anger that flushed his face. The muscles
tensed at the corners of his jaws as he grabbed the reins
and jerked them out of Clift's hands.

Clift staggered and then recovered. He came up angrily
with his fist. It glanced off the side of Denny's head. He
dropped the reins and both horses, startled, jumped back
and stood watching, their ears pointed at the sparring
boys. Denny ducked another blow, stumbled, but struggled
quickly to his feet and swung wildly. The blow slid off
Clift's shoulder shoving him back but he recovered and
for a few seconds they traded punch for punch, pummeling
each other with short jabs that did nothing but spend
their energy.

They separated, measured their arm reach, leaned toward each other, and then Clift dove in. He missed. A
surprised look flooded his features. The horses snorted
and moved aside. Denny followed and then they closed in
again, smashing each other in the ribs with short jabs that
drew grunts from both. Clift had the bigger bulk, the
longer reach, but Denny was quick. Clift reached for his
leg. Denny growled and kicked him loose. Clift wheezed
and his wind was short. Both boys were tiring. They
paused, glaring at each other, breathing in great gulps of
air, measuring for the next move. Denny's chest heaved
and he stood spraddle-legged, waiting. Clift leaped and
Denny, narrowing his eyes, gave a solid poke with his left.
Clift's head shot back as the blow smashed onto the point
of his nose. He grunted and sat down hard. He wiped a

47

hand across his nose gingerly, and sat looking at the smear of blood across his wrist.

"Now do you want to lead the way?" Denny gasped, going back on his heels, his fists steadied for the next attack. Clift stayed where he was. "Get—up. And get on your horse." He watched while Clift got slowly to his feet, still wiping at his nose. He waited while Clift gathered the reins and tried to ease up to the nervous horse. When he was mounted, Denny put his hands down, brushed the dust from his clothes, picked up his hat, hit it across his arm, and settled it firmly on his head. He still glared at Clift, who now regarded him uneasily. "We're going to find Freddie. When we get back to the stables you're going to tell Sam Kendall that you led Freddie away on purpose." Clift was silent. He felt of his nose, his fingers gently touching the reddened bridge. They started back along the trail toward the opening in the rock.

They passed the opening and Denny stopped to study the ground. They climbed steadily, with the trail getting steeper and narrowing where the rocks jutted out, until they were forced to take one leg out of the stirrup to keep from scraping against the rough ledges. Then the trail widened again where one ridge left to join another.

They waded through more brush and came out on a small clearing. There stood Freddie's horse, quiet, his head low. He jerked his head up with his ears pointed and nickered a greeting. The reins were wrapped loosely around a branch. Denny stopped, scanned the surrounding rocks, searched the steep sides of the hill. Freddie was not in sight. A rock, the size of a small shed, loomed up in front of them, completely blocking the trail. To one side, as if they had been rolled like marbles down a trough, were smaller rocks with scraggly wisps of brush and grass growing out of the cracks.

"He must have gone up through those rocks," Denny mused aloud.

"You'd better wait for the posse," Clift muttered soberly. He sat humped over, the fight gone out of him.

"We'll get him ourselves," Denny stated. Clift shrugged his shoulders without argument. "I'll climb up there and you stay here," said Denny. Clift's answer was a grunt and he kept his eyes averted. He felt his nose again, snuffing carefully.

Denny swung down and tied Blaze beside Freddie's horse. He grabbed a twisted shrub for a handhold and began to pull himself up over the rocks. He tested each hold as he pulled on the tough branches and looked into each crack as he passed. When he gained the top he stood up and scanned the area closely.

"I don't see him," he called down. Clift ignored him and didn't raise his head. Denny studied the land below.

From this vantage point he could see the whole canyon. Over the farthest ridge he could see part of the pasture. Denny cupped his hands and called. No answer. Denny started to climb down on the other side.

"Freddie!" He stopped to listen. "Freddie!" Faintly he heard a call somewhere among the maze of branches. "Freddie, answer me," Denny shouted. The faint voice came again. He cocked his head trying to place the position of the sound. Sliding and half jumping down the steep incline, Denny probed every inch of the terrain, looking

49

for any sign of movement. The leaves moved with the slight breeze but nothing took shape.

"Wave your arms, I can't see you," Denny called. The voice came again and Denny began to follow the sound. He grabbed a small branch of a tree and swung himself around a protruding rock.

"Hey, here I am." Freddie's voice sounded right beside him. Denny stopped. He studied every rock, every bush. "Up here." Freddie looked as if he were dangling from a fishing pole. "I'm caught. I started to slide and grabbed this bush. I flipped and a piece of branch went under my belt. It's pressing into my back. I can't reach it."

"Why did you come down on this side?" Denny wanted to know.

"I thought I could see the stable from here and get my bearings," Freddie explained. "Where's Clift?" His blond hair was sprinkled with leaves and somewhere he had lost his hat. His jeans pulled tightly across his thighs like a sling. His legs swung almost free of the rock and if he put his arms back he could steady himself somewhat. A tough, sinewy branch of chaparral was thrust under-

EVEREN RAYMOND KINSTLER

neath the tight belt and turned upward against Freddie's back. Against his weight it was like a firm but limber hook. The pressure kept it from slipping free of the belt. "Why isn't Clift here to help me get down?"

"He's on the other side of this rock," Denny said. "Mr. Kendall's getting a posse. I have to get you back before they start out to look for you. Why didn't you holler sooner?"

"I did," Freddie told him. "But no one answered. I thought everyone had gone and left me." Freddie squirmed with useless effort. "Get me out of here. Is Mr. Kendall mad?"

"Of course he's mad," Denny growled— "at me for not bringing you back."

"I was sure scared," Freddie said grimly. "I kicked until I was tired but the more I kicked the tighter my belt got. My back hurts. Get me down, Denny."

"I'd better get Clift to help." Denny studied Freddie's position. "I can't reach you."

"That Clift," Freddie muttered. "He said he knew all about this canyon. He dared me to come up here." He squirmed again. "Come on, Denny, it's going to get dark pretty soon."

Denny pulled himself up and disappeared over the top of the rock again. He edged his way around until he could look down. Blaze and Freddie's horse stood chewing lazily on the green saplings that grew at the base of the rock. Clift was not in sight, nor was his horse. Denny frowned and looked about with some indecision. He finally climbed down until he reached Blaze's side. He untied the coil of rope fastened to the saddle and, slipping it over his arm, started up the incline again.

When he could see Freddie again he stopped to rest and uncoiled the length of rope.

"Where's Clift?" Freddie steadied himself with his fingers pressed hard against the rock. He grimaced as the movement poked the branch into his back.

"He's not here," was all Denny could say.

"How're you going to get me down from here alone?" Freddie's forehead wrinkled with worry. "I'll freeze if I have to stay here all night."

"I don't know," Denny told him. He looked about and studied the rock, the nearby tree, and fingered the rope thoughtfully. "Maybe I can get a loop around you and pull you down."

"I can't get my feet against the rock, they slip," Freddie said.

"Here," Denny called. "I'm going to throw the rope to you." He gathered it in loops. "Grab it and tie it around your waist."

Denny tossed the rope and Freddie grabbed and inched it around his waist. He tied a square knot. "Now what?"

"I'll have to get it over that branch, up there," Denny explained. "Maybe if I take the pressure off your belt you can unfasten it." Denny scrambled to the base of the tree and braced himself underneath. He tossed the rope as hard as he could but it fell short. He looked about for a rock to tie the rope around. The rope was stiff but he managed to make it firm enough to hold. He tossed it again but it struck a branch and the rock loosened and fell to the ground, rolling away down the slope. "I guess I'll have to climb the doggone tree."

Tying the end of the rope around his waist, Denny grasped the tree with his legs and arms and started easing himself up. Twice he lost his hold and slid down to the base.

"You'll never get up there," Freddie whined. "This branch is poking a hole right in my back."

Denny took another breath and tried again. He eased up slowly, clamping his legs tightly as he moved his arms up. Inch by inch he moved up the rough bark until his fingers found a small branch to grasp. Straining and pulling, he braced himself against the trunk and pulled himself up and over the limb. He tossed the rope over the limb and slid down again.

"Now, when I tighten this rope see if you can reach your belt," Denny ordered. He pulled with all his strength. Freddie's arms pulled against the rope as he tried to reach the belt. "See if you can lean against the rope and brace your feet on the rock," Denny directed. "That should take the strain off the branch. Can't you reach back and pull the thing out?"

Freddie struggled to get his feet against the rock. He slipped and swung around. "You'll have to pull me higher," Freddie said. Denny hung on to the rope and put all his weight on it. Freddie pulled at the belt. It was awkward. The stem of the buckle refused to pull out of the hole in the belt. Freddie took a deep breath and pulled again. Denny let the rope down slowly. As the tension relieved the pressure on the branch the belt loosened until it pulled out of the loops and suddenly Freddie slid and tumbled down the face of the rock. Denny fought to ease his fall.

"Gosh, I scraped my hands on that rock," Freddie complained. "Come on, let's get out of here."

They climbed around the rock and down where the horses were tied.

"What are you going to do about Clift?" Freddie asked. Denny didn't answer. He studied the ground for prints and after he untied Blaze he followed them on foot. They reached the split in the rock and Denny stopped.

"His tracks lead right to the entrance," Denny said. "He's gone on down." They went through the archlike rock and started on down the trail. When they could see the stables Freddie pointed to the group of saddled horses tied at the hitching rails. The parking lot was full of cars with trailers. Men milled about the stableyard.

"That looks like Clift down there." Freddie pointed to the familiar figure talking to Sam Kendall. "What do you suppose he's saying?"

"Nothing good," Denny commented. "He's probably fixed me good." They watched Clift following Sam Kendall about the yard as the horses were backed out of the trailers and saddled. Denny urged Blaze into a trot. As they came down the lane Denny saw Claudia wheel her bicycle to a stop and shove it around a corner of the barn. "I'll see you later," he called to Freddie and galloped around the barn as Claudia leaned over a stable door to stroke the nose of a black horse. A slim middle-aged woman with heavy-lensed glasses stood with her.

"Claudia, what are you doing down here?" Denny called.

Claudia turned. "Oh, hi, Denny," she greeted him. "I just came down to ride home with you. Mom thought you ought to be home earlier than this."

"Yes, I know," Denny said grimly. "I have to go see Mr. Kendall."

"Denny, this is Miss Butterfield." Claudia indicated the mousy-haired woman beside her. "She is going to buy Domino."

"Isn't he beautiful?" Miss Butterfield nodded to Denny and smoothed the dark muzzle. "He's quite a handful but I'm sure I'll be able to handle him."

"He's a nice horse," Denny said quietly, without interest. "We have to get home, Claudia."

"Are we going right now?" Claudia walked over and put her face against Blaze's muzzle.

"I want to see Mr. Kendall first." Denny frowned. He climbed out of the saddle and, leading Blaze, walked slowly toward the stableyard.

"Are you coming tomorrow, Miss Butterfield?" Claudia called back over her shoulder.

"I've been here every day," Miss Butterfield answered. "I'll see the owner tomorrow." She left the door and stepped along with Claudia. Domino whinnied and they heard him kick at the wall as he tossed his head in their direction. "I think he knows me already."

"You start home and I'll be along," Denny called back over his shoulder. Claudia looked at him in surprise. She slowed, smiled at Miss Butterfield, and then took the bicycle where it leaned against the wall, pushing it in front of her.

When Denny reached the stableyard Sam Kendall was

standing, arms akimbo, listening to Freddie. The men were unsaddling their horses.

"He's lying!" Clift glared angrily at Freddie.

"I am not," Freddie insisted. "Clift said it would be all right if I went with him—"

Sam Kendall turned away. "I don't want to hear any more about it."

"But I'm just trying to tell you what happened," Freddie said anxiously. "I didn't mean to do anything wrong...."

"I'll tend to you later." Sam Kendall stopped talking when he saw Denny. "I suppose you have a story, too?"

"No, sir," Denny said quietly. Sam Kendall's eyes were bright with anger. An explanation would be of little use.

A man in uniform came up to Mr. Kendall. "I guess we'll be going." He smiled at Denny. "It looks like this young fellow took care of everything. If we ever need a guide into the canyon I'll get in touch with you."

"I'm sorry to have called you out on a false alarm," Sam Kendall apologized.

"Thanks, sir," Denny murmured. "I guess I'd better go." He watched the expression on Sam Kendall's face. It wasn't friendly.

Sam Kendall was unsmiling. "Wait a minute. I owe you some money."

"That's all right, Mr. Kendall. Just forget it," Denny said.

"No, let's get it settled." Mr. Kendall pulled out his wallet. "Let's see. At fifty cents per person, that's three dollars." He counted the money out into Denny's hand.

He put the wallet away and walked off. Denny stood where he left him. Claudia shoved her bicycle up beside him.

"I thought I told you to start home." Denny's face was pale. He watched Sam Kendall, but Mr. Kendall didn't make any attempt to speak to him again.

"It's getting dark," Claudia complained.

"I could take you home in my car," Miss Butterfield offered.

"Oh, no, thanks, I'll ride along beside Blaze," Claudia answered.

"Then I'll be going," Miss Butterfield said. "I'll be back tomorrow, Mr. Kendall," she called after him.

Sam Kendall turned to look after her. He shook his head. "Problems, problems, if it isn't kids, it's horses." He viewed them all with distaste. Denny turned away from his angry eyes. Denny mounted Blaze and motioned Claudia to follow him. There was nothing to do but go home.

6. THE BOARDER

CLAUDIA went out to groom Blaze after breakfast. Denny strolled out to the stable, looked at Cricket eating, then came over to watch Claudia.

"Where're you goin'?" Denny brushed a twig out of Blaze's mane.

"I'm going to ride down to Kendall's stable," she said. "Come on, help me saddle, so we can go."

"I'm not going down there any more." Denny's voice was sharp.

"If you stay away," Claudia said anxiously, "he'll think you're afraid."

"I'm not afraid!" Denny snapped.

"Well, then," Claudia began on a stern note, "let's go down to prove you're not." Denny regarded her warily and then tightened the cinch firmly. "Do you think he's mad at you because of the trail ride?"

"I don't think he wants me around any more," Denny said. "I had a job to do and I failed."

"It wasn't your fault," Claudia said.

"Maybe not," Denny agreed. "But it didn't look right for me."

"Well." Claudia shook her head. "It won't look right if you avoid Mr. Kendall." She waited. Denny stared at

59

her for a long moment and then mounted Blaze. He pulled her up behind him. Blaze started off at a slow trot.

Denny and Claudia heard the man talking to Sam Kendall as they walked up to the shed row. After they tied Blaze, Claudia skipped ahead but Denny walked hesitantly, almost reluctant for Mr. Kendall to see him. But when Sam Kendall did notice him he nodded his head in solemn greeting and then gave his attention to the man beside him. Claudia skipped up beside Sam Kendall and peered up into the face of the stranger.

"This Miss Butterfield, she's an old-maid schoolteacher," he was explaining to Mr. Kendall. "Got an inheritance or something. Wants to buy Domino." He took a few puffs on his pipe before he knocked the ashes out and ground them into the dirt with the ball of his foot, then pocketed his pipe. His narrow, faded eyes set in the fat wrinkles of his pink face scrutinized Sam Kendall's eyes. He tapped Sam's arm. "A little commission for you too."

"You ought to get him out of here so she can't see him." Sam Kendall gave him a stern glance. "Domino's no horse for a lady." Denny eased up and looked at the black gelding. He was beautiful. His coat glistened like satin and with every roll of the alert brown eyes, the white showed, promising a bit of wildness. His ears pointed and he snorted at each object he saw. "He'll kick every chance he gets."

"Isn't he wonderful?" Claudia was enchanted. Sam Kendall ran his hand along the horse's side and gingerly reached forward and picked up a rear foot. Domino snorted and jerked, but Mr. Kendall's heavy arms bulged and he held the foot tightly. "Buck, this horse shouldn't be sold to a woman. If you don't sell him today you'll have to move him out of my stable."

"Aw, now listen, Sam," Buck protested and drew back blinking.

"I wouldn't even board him," Sam said harshly. "He kicked two boards off the stall wall last night."

"I know he kicks," Buck said. "But I gotta sell him. I need a payment for my car." Buck lifted his hat and ran a nervous hand through the matted gray hair. He moved closer to Domino and without warning a hoof flashed through the air. Even though Buck was far enough away to miss the blow he flinched. "You black devil!" he snarled.

"I'm going to tell Miss Butterfield not to buy this horse," Sam warned. "She'll want to board it here and I can't take care of it."

"I ain't never gone against you, Sam." Buck bit off the words. "Now you keep outa my business." He shifted uneasily as Sam regarded him with distaste. "I'll take my chances with this schoolteacher."

"Oh, you won't have to," Claudia broke in. "She wants him anyway, even if he does kick." Sam Kendall directed his gaze, first at Denny and then at Claudia. "Mr. Kendall, if Miss Butterfield buys Domino and you won't board him, do you care if we do?"

"Claudia, you don't want anything to do with that horse," Sam Kendall told her. "He's been spoiled and he doesn't respect anyone." He put a hand on her shoulder. "I wouldn't want you to get hurt." Sam glared at Buck. "Do you see what could happen?"

"But Uncle Tom would know what to do," Claudia assured them.

"No doubt," Sam Kendall agreed. "But who has the time or the inclination to retrain Domino?" He shook his head. "She still shouldn't buy him."

"He's so beautiful. How could she help not wanting him?" Claudia eyed the horse with admiration and Domino tossed his head and nickered.

"He's real horseflesh, all right," Sam Kendall agreed. "But what good is he if no one can handle him without the chance of getting kicked?" Claudia was quiet.

She stood and watched Buck brush the black coat. When he started on the hind quarters he tied one front foot to Domino's halter. "Why did he do that?" Claudia whispered to Denny.

"He might fall down if he tries to kick," Denny answered. Buck regarded them grimly. "When he brushes the other side he'll tie the front foot on that side," Denny added. "Domino is so busy trying to balance he can't kick."

Buck finished the grooming and led Domino around the stableyard. Claudia and Denny stepped back under the shed row when a car drove in and two women got out. One was Miss Butterfield. She adjusted her glasses and peered up at Buck when he gave her a cordial greeting. Then Buck led Domino in a trot so she could watch him. He turned and brought the horse to a stop in front of them.

"This is Miss Alice Brown. She has a dancing school and she wants a horse too," she said.

"Fine, fine." Buck smiled broadly. "I can find you a horse. This one is a very spirited animal." He smiled across at Denny and Claudia. "Of course, I have another party who wants him ..."

Miss Butterfield rose to the bait. "This is the one I want ... I've already decided."

"But Agatha," Miss Brown protested, "have you ridden him yet?"

"No." Miss Butterfield raised her eyebrows. "But I'm going to buy him." She paused. "I know he's spirited. I shall have to learn to handle him." She stared at Alice Brown. "Now, Alice, don't try to change my mind."

"Well, I want a horse I can ride right away." Miss Brown walked around Domino looking him over carefully. "He's beautiful, all right, but you can have him. I hope you know what you're doing."

"He'll be such a challenge." Miss Butterfield began petting Domino on the nose. She ran her hand over the satin neck and on down the smooth back. Denny drew a sharp breath as her fingers ran over the rounded hip bone. She moved close beside him, smoothing his leg down beside the hock. Sam Kendall walked up and Denny could see the concern on his face. No one spoke. Buck scratched his chin and held tightly to the lead rope. Claudia was chewing on her thumb. Suddenly Domino cow-kicked, shoving Miss Butterfield off balance. The thick-lensed glasses flew six feet away. Miss Butterfield staggered to regain her feet and Denny reached out a hand to support her. He saw the angry glance that Sam threw at Buck. Claudia ran to pick up the glasses, caught Miss Butterfield's hand, and pressed them within her grasp. It was plain she couldn't see without them. She adjusted them and flushed with embarrassment.

"Are you hurt?" Sam's voice was half anger and half concern.

"No, no, Domino just kicked my glasses off ... that is ... he shoved me. He didn't touch me at all. I guess I shouldn't have been so hasty." She smiled bravely at all of them. "He's a spirited beast but I shall tame him."

"Oh, Agatha, you're being foolish." Alice Brown took her arm and started easing her away. "You can't buy that awful horse."

"How you talk, Alice!" Miss Butterfield pulled her arm away. She stubbornly flattened her wispy hair back over her ears and straightened her thin shoulders. "You'd think I'd never been around a horse. If it's the last thing I ever do I'll tame him." She bit her lip and stood defiantly in front of Alice Brown. Claudia grinned at Denny and he looked at Miss Butterfield with new respect. Sam glared at Buck as Miss Butterfield took out her check book.

"Maybe ... maybe you'd better let me find you another horse." Buck regarded Sam nervously and tightened his hold on Domino's halter.

"I should say not." Miss Butterfield hurriedly wrote the check and handed it to Buck with a flourish. "I'm looking forward to this." She smiled at Sam. "Now about a stall. ..."

"I'm sorry, Miss Butterfield." Sam plunged his hands in his pockets. "I have no stall for Domino."

"Oh, dear." Miss Butterfield adjusted her glasses again and stared around the small circle uneasily. "What shall I do?"

"You can board Domino at our stable," Claudia broke in.

"Claudia!" Denny snapped in a loud whisper.

"Well, she can," Claudia insisted. Denny sighed and kicked a stone out of his path. He opened his mouth to speak, but Miss Butterfield was looking at him. The muscle at the corner of his set jaw gave indication that he wanted to voice his thoughts but he took a deep breath, pressed his lips tightly together, and looked away.

"Are you sure it's all right?" Miss Butterfield wrinkled her forehead. "Is it far from here?"

"About a mile, I guess," Claudia told her. "We have a new stall ready and a nice pasture."

"Well, that's settled then." Miss Butterfield turned to Buck. "You can get the address from Claudia and please make out a bill of sale for me." She smiled at Claudia. "I'll be over this evening and see Domino settled in his new home." She waved at them all airily and taking the scowling Miss Brown by the arm she propelled her toward the car and drove off.

Denny took Claudia by the arm and pulled her around. "Why did you tell her we'd board that horse?" Denny dropped her arm as she jerked away. "You know it isn't smart to have a horse nobody else wants."

"Buck, I ought to sock you in the jaw," they heard Sam say as he led Domino away.

Claudia watched them disappear behind the barn. "You just wait until Uncle Tom sees him," Claudia said quickly. "He'll know what to do." Denny's eyes darkened. "You want to keep the ranch, don't you?" she added.

"You heard Mr. Kendall say he kicks everything to

pieces," Denny said grimly. "We haven't even enough money to build new stalls. How do you think we're going to be able to keep repairing?"

"Oh, we'll do something," Claudia countered confidently. She studied his face and then smiling up at him she took his hand. "Come on, Denny, we have to go home and get the stall ready." Denny stood for a moment. Without speaking he put his arm around her shoulders and they walked slowly to where Blaze was tied. He climbed into the saddle and pulled her up behind him and they turned toward home.

Uncle Tom passed them in the pickup truck as they reached the driveway and was waiting for them when they rode into the yard.

"She's done it again, Uncle Tom," Denny called.

"Done what?" Uncle Tom grinned up at Claudia. She wrinkled her nose at him and jumped down.

"She got us a boarder," Denny said. "A kicking boarder."

"How do you stop a horse from kicking, Uncle Tom?" Claudia interrupted. "Domino kicks people and stalls and everything."

"Now why did you take a horse like that?" Uncle Tom sobered and his glance sought Denny's.

"No one else would have him, that's why," Denny muttered.

"Well, we had to get a boarder," Claudia said. "And besides it's forty dollars a month." Denny explained how Domino had kicked Miss Butterfield and how her glasses had been jarred off her face. "He only really shoved her, though," Claudia finished.

"They shouldn't have sold that horse to a woman," Uncle Tom said, shaking his head. "Well, we'll see what can be done."

"Miss Butterfield wanted the horse anyhow," Claudia said. "All we have to do is teach Domino not to kick." Claudia took Uncle Tom's hand and swung it back and forth. "You can, can't you?"

"Well, it looks like we're going to have to." Uncle Tom took his pipe from his pocket, packed the tobacco in it slowly and firmly. He looked off into space thoughtfully and Claudia studied his face and waited. Denny put Blaze away and came over as Uncle Tom puffed great clouds of smoke into the air. "Now, where's that collar you bought for Blue? Denny, I'll need about a foot of chain, heavy chain."

"I'll get the collar." Claudia turned. "Blue doesn't need a collar anyhow."

"I guess I can get the chain we were going to use on the new gate," Denny put in.

When Buck drove into the yard with Domino stomping in the trailer, Blaze and Cricket had been moved to the unfinished stalls. They watched Buck unload the black horse. He backed quickly down the ramp and snorted at everything around him. He minced warily about, his finely chiseled head, broad and intelligent, held high as he smelled the air.

"Isn't he wonderful, Uncle Tom?" Claudia clasped her hands together.

"He is a beauty," Uncle Tom said admiringly. "Well bred, too, must be thoroughbred."

"He's extra fine," Buck said. "Bred from good running stock." He hesitated. "Needs some work, though." He glanced quickly at Claudia and Denny. "Kicks a little."

Uncle Tom took Domino by the lead rope and tied him to the rail fence. Buck wasted no more time. He banged the tail gate into place and rattled out of the driveway in a cloud of dust.

Uncle Tom ran a practiced hand over the well-knit shoulders and down the deep barrel.

"Denny, I want you to take Domino out in the corral," Uncle Tom told him. "We might as well start now. I'll put the chain and collar on his leg and we're going to need plenty of room because he isn't going to like it." Uncle Tom put the collar through a link of chain. "Now, which leg does he kick with?"

"The left one," Denny spoke up.

"No, he didn't," Claudia argued. "Miss Butterfield was

standing on the right side of the horse when she was petting him.''

"We'll try the right hind leg," Uncle Tom said. He
moved toward Domino. "Hold his right front leg up while
I put the collar in place." Denny pulled the right front leg
up tight against his thigh and held on to Domino's halter.

"See." Claudia jumped up and down in excitement.
"See, Uncle Tom knows how to get him off balance. He
knows all about horses, more than Buck even." Uncle Tom
chuckled at her enthusiasm as he eased toward Domino's
rear and gently placed the dog collar firmly above the
hock. Domino snorted and tried to pull his front leg from
Denny's grasp but he held tightly until Uncle Tom nodded.

When the collar was buckled in place Denny stepped back quickly and handed the lead rope to Uncle Tom.

Domino stood for a moment and looked at them. His ears flicked uncertainly and then he moved. The chain dangled against his leg and suddenly he jumped and kicked out. The chain whipped around and cracked his leg brutally. He kicked angrily. His eyes rolled wildly as he reared and then whirled. Uncle Tom followed him about the corral as Domino fought to get away from the whipping of the chain. Then he stopped. He stood still, snorting, quivering as he looked around at them. His ears moved like twin semaphores. He lifted his foot and then set it down again.

"He'll find out that when he doesn't kick he won't get hurt," Uncle Tom explained.

"It really hurts." Claudia looked worried.

"Well," Uncle Tom admitted, "he is punishing himself."

"Yea." Denny grinned. "When he decides not to kick he won't get hurt any more." He led Domino toward the stall. The black lifted his collared leg as if he were walking on eggs.

"We'll leave this on until he is afraid to kick. It will only take a day or two before he connects being hurt with kicking. He'll probably never kick again," Uncle Tom explained. "If he does, then we just repeat this treatment."

"Uncle Tom, you know everything." Claudia smiled up at him.

"Well, I know a little." Uncle Tom was pleased. "Bad habits should not be allowed to grow. It takes a little time and patience."

70

"I guess most people don't want to be bothered," Denny mused.

Domino started munching hay but he was careful how he stepped around.

As they walked to the house a coupé drove into the yard, and Miss Butterfield stepped out. "I came to see Domino," she said. Miss Butterfield glanced about. "This is very nice." She walked to the corral and glanced into the stall. "Domino, Domino," she called. Domino snorted and stepped back. The chain rattled as he kicked out. It cracked against his leg. He stopped and stood spraddle-legged, trembling. "What have you done to him?" Miss Butterfield whirled and fixed all of them angrily.

"He is a kicking horse, Miss Butterfield," Uncle Tom said patiently. "We're going to train him not to kick."

"I will not have my horse abused," Miss Butterfield cried loudly. She nervously pushed a wisp of mousy hair behind her ear. "Take that off at once!"

"We didn't do anything but put the chain on," Denny told her. "He's the one who does the beating."

"If the horse stays here then it will not be allowed to kick," Uncle Tom said evenly.

"Then I shall certainly move him somewhere else." Miss Butterfield's voice rose to an angry pitch. "I shall find another stable immediately and have him moved."

The children's mother came out the back door. Denny knew by the expression on her face that she had heard Miss Butterfield's angry voice. Mary Wolff walked with quick steps and she stopped in front of Miss Butterfield. "Perhaps you'd like to use our telephone," she said sharply.

Miss Butterfield stared at her and thrust her chin out. "Thank you, I will!" She followed Mary stiffly and Uncle Tom trailed along behind.

"Well, there goes your boarder," Denny said to Claudia.

"It's just as well," Uncle Tom said quietly over his shoulder. "You can't afford to have a kicking horse around. He'll kick Blaze and Cricket and even you. You won't be able to trust him at any time unless he's stopped now."

"I was hoping we had a boarder at last." Claudia thrust her fists into her jeans. "Everything was going to be fine."

"I told you it wouldn't work." Denny stared at her coldly. "It isn't as easy as you think to save the ranch. I don't think we'll save it at all. Nothing we've tried has worked. We might as well give up."

"You never give up, Denny," Uncle Tom assured him. "When you fail it is only a sign that you've tried." Uncle Tom held the door open and they went inside. Miss Butterfield was thumbing through the yellow pages of the telephone book. Their mother stood leaning against the sinkboard, her arms folded, a grim expression on her face.

"Well, this isn't the only boarder in the world," Claudia whispered to Denny. "I'll get another one." Denny frowned at her and they all stood quietly, watching Miss Butterfield. She ran her finger down the page and then picked up the receiver. They watched her dial the number and its whir was the only sound in the room. Suddenly the sound of splintering wood rent the air. Miss Butterfield looked startled and put the receiver back on its cradle as Denny and Claudia banged out the back door in the direc-

THE BOARDER

tion of the stable. Miss Butterfield hurried after them, and Uncle Tom and their mother followed.

The door of the stable hung from one hinge and Domino was sending sharp, short kicks in the direction of the wall as he fought the chain on his leg.

"He'll kick our stable down!" Denny cried and ran to the gate.

"Wait, Denny," Uncle Tom called after him, "let me get him." He opened the gate and talked sternly to the nodding black head in the doorway. Domino blew and then snorted defiantly. Uncle Tom reached his head and then quickly grasped his halter. He led the black out of the stable, through the gate, and tied him to the rail fence. "Now, if you want to finish your call, we'll leave him tied out here where he can't tear things up. Of course, you'll have to pay for the repairs," he solemnly told Miss Butterfield.

"The collar slipped down," Denny announced. "It's loose around his ankle."

"I guess I should have had it tighter," Uncle Tom told him.

"Would that collar and chain really stop him from kicking?" Miss Butterfield looked at Uncle Tom with a sideways glance.

"It usually works," Uncle Tom commented. "Some horses are harder to break than others. Domino has never been taught to mind. He needs to be retrained. He's a superbly bred animal but at this moment I wouldn't give you five cents for him."

"I think you should get him moved before dark," Mrs. Wolff suggested.

Miss Butterfield studied them. Her face was no longer flushed with anger. "I'm afraid I owe you all an apology," she began. "I guess I should be glad to have someone help me break a spoiled horse. After my bad behavior would you reconsider and let him stay?"

Uncle Tom looked at Mrs. Wolff. The children watched her face with anxiety. "If Uncle Tom thinks it is all right, then I'll agree," she said.

"Any horse can be retrained if you have the patience," Uncle Tom said.

"I'll be glad to pay for any training," Miss Butterfield said.

"I don't think we should keep him," Denny began.

"We'll be careful," Claudia interrupted. "He's too beautiful to let someone else have him. Uncle Tom will know what to do."

"I'm leaving it entirely up to Uncle Tom," their mother said.

"Then the first thing we'll do is put the chain back on," Uncle Tom ordered. "This time we'll see that it doesn't come off." Denny ran to recover the collar and chain which had finally been kicked off and were lying near the gate. Miss Butterfield took out her check book to pay for the board. Claudia's eyes were bright as she handed it to her.

"Thank you, Miss Butterfield," she said. "I have a new horse to train. Maybe we can do it together."

"I'd like that," Miss Butterfield said. "I know I've lots to learn."

"Of course, Cricket doesn't kick," Claudia said evenly.

"But I have to find out what she will do when I climb on her back for the first time."

"Then, why don't we start tomorrow?" Miss Butterfield said quickly.

7. THE TRAINERS

WHEN Miss Butterfield drove into the yard the next afternoon after school Claudia was already grooming Cricket. In just a few days a difference could be seen in the little mare. The warm spring weather was causing her to shed and the satiny dark dapple of her bay coat was beginning to show underneath the winter hair.

"She's going to be a pretty little thing." Miss Butterfield regarded the slim rump that was starting to fill out. "She has a head like an Arabian." Denny and Uncle Tom came around the corner of the stable, and all three watched Claudia brush Cricket's sides with long sweeping motions.

"A good grooming is worth a pound of feed," Uncle Tom commented.

"Well, Claudia had better do a lot of grooming then,"

Denny said quickly. "Because we're going to need hay again soon."

"Oh, we'll get it when the time comes," Claudia said evenly.

"We'd better take the board money and put in a supply of hay," Denny suggested.

"No." Claudia stopped her grooming and was unusually serious. "We'll have enough from my baby sitting and your lawn cutting to buy hay. This money is for the ranch."

"I think Claudia is right," Uncle Tom spoke up.

"Well, we do have enough to buy another ton," Denny admitted.

"How is Domino?" Miss Butterfield turned toward the stable.

"I think you'd better handle him from the ground today and give him a chance to get acquainted with you," Uncle Tom explained. "And every time he makes a wrong move, scold him."

"Oh, I shall," Miss Butterfield agreed. "I want to learn to train a horse." She smiled. "I've done a lot of riding but every horse I've ever ridden was already trained."

"Domino must learn to respect your disapproval," Uncle Tom went on. "When he is good, pet him and let him know you like him. He'll get so he'll look for your affection." Uncle Tom led the black horse out of the stableyard and tied him at the rail fence. "Leave the collar and chain on until you have finished grooming him."

Miss Butterfield took the rubber currycomb and began a vigorous circular motion of brushing that loosened the winter hair until the air was thick with it flying around the yard.

"You have to keep your mouth closed and your eyes squinted so you won't get full of hair, don't you?" Claudia mumbled between tight lips.

"Goodness, yes." Miss Butterfield blew her breath out through her mouth. "Phew! I'll be glad when all the winter hair is gone. Are you going to ride your horse today?"

"Yes," Claudia said. "Uncle Tom made me an Indian bridle out of rawhide. Cricket is so gentle I don't think she will do anything wrong."

"What is an Indian bridle?" Miss Butterfield wanted to know.

"It's a long piece of rawhide that has a loop at one end," Claudia explained. "You slip the loop over the lower jaw and use the rest for a rein."

"That doesn't seem like much to hold a horse," Miss Butterfield said.

"Uncle Tom says you can handle a tough horse with an Indian bridle." Claudia smiled at Uncle Tom. She stopped to pat Cricket's muzzle as the little mare explored her shirt pocket with her nose.

Miss Butterfield started brushing Domino vigorously with the stiff brush. As she worked toward his rear he laid his ears back and raised his leg. The chain dangled, and he put the leg down.

"No!" Miss Butterfield slapped him smartly on the neck. He stiffened and stood still while she finished the grooming. "He's learning already what no means." Miss Butterfield was pleased. "I wonder if your Uncle Tom

would ride Domino for me so I can see just what he does."
She turned to Uncle Tom. He nodded.

"Uncle Tom can do anything with a horse," Denny
spoke up.

"I'll try him for you," Uncle Tom said. "Denny, get
your saddle and Blaze's bridle."

"I have a flat saddle. But I have to buy a bridle for
Domino." Miss Butterfield stepped back and looked at
the smooth coat. "There now, that's enough for today."

Uncle Tom placed the saddle on Domino's back and
quickly tightened the cinch. After he had fastened the
throat latch of the bridle he had Denny hold up the black's
front leg while he removed the collar and chain. Domino
pranced and minced his steps, but he seemed to respect
Uncle Tom's firmness on the reins and stood still when
Uncle Tom eased gently into the saddle. He danced off
sideways, holding his head proudly.

"Look at him dance," Claudia cried. "He acts like a
parade horse."

"This horse was well trained once," Uncle Tom called
as he turned Domino quickly, first in one direction and
then in the other. Domino changed leads and cantered
evenly. "Here, Miss Butterfield, try him."

"Don't you think I should get better acquainted with
him? You said ..." Miss Butterfield began.

Uncle Tom climbed down and handed her the reins.
"Keep a firm but light rein on him. I believe he likes to
work. I think kicking is his only fault. No doubt he's been
teased and has been confined to a stall too much."

"If you think it's all right." Miss Butterfield swung
into the saddle and took Domino around the yard, putting

78

him through his gaits with a practiced hand. She smiled at them all. "He's just what I've always wanted. Now, Claudia, it's your turn."

"Do you mean you would let me ride Domino?" Claudia's eyes were bright.

"He handles like a baby," Miss Butterfield said.

"Blaze is the only big horse I've ever been on," Claudia admitted.

"See how Domino handles," Uncle Tom said. "Then you'll know what to strive for with Cricket." Claudia climbed into the saddle and took Domino around the yard. She handled him easily and when she brought him back and climbed down Miss Butterfield handed the reins to Denny. Domino handled just as well for Denny.

"I figured out a surcingle for you, Claudia." Uncle Tom went over to his pickup truck and reached in the back to pull out two cinches. He fastened them together with a leather latigo. He placed a blanket on Cricket's back and put one cinch across the blanket. He brought it around Cricket's barrel and fastened the ends of the cinches together with another latigo, tightening it to hold the blankets firmly on Cricket's back. "This is a homemade surcingle but it will do until you get a saddle." He slipped the rawhide loop over the little mare's jaw and handed the single rein to Claudia. "Walk her and see how she reins." He gave Claudia a leg up and she gave Cricket a slight kick as she urged her forward.

Cricket mouthed the rawhide thong, but it was on the bars of her mouth so that her teeth couldn't touch it. Claudia was awkward with the single rein but soon began to learn to pull it slightly to turn the mare right and to lay it across her neck to guide her left.

"She needs a lot of work," Denny commented.

"She probably was just started," Uncle Tom said.

"As soon as I'm accustomed to Domino we'll ride out together," Miss Butterfield said. "We both need to go slowly with our horses."

Blaze nickered from the pasture and trotted up to the fence to look at them. Cricket answered him, and Claudia jumped off and started to unfasten the surcingle.

"I'm going to let Cricket have a run," Claudia said.

She led Cricket to the pasture gate and turned her in.
Blaze snorted and bucked. Cricket jumped straight in the
air and twisted her body, then the two horses raced around

the pasture, heads high and tails flying straight out. They came to a high-trotted stop at the gate and blew and whistled. "Aren't they silly?" Claudia laughed at them and climbed on the fence to watch.

Domino snorted and pawed as he watched the two horses at play. "He wants to be out there too," Miss Butterfield said. "Could I turn him in with the others? He's probably never had anyone to play with."

"Here, I'll unsaddle him for you." Uncle Tom untied the latigo and pulled the saddle from Domino's back. He put the halter over the impatient nose and led him to the pasture gate. When he found himself free Domino dug his feet into the turf and galloped madly around the pasture with Cricket and Blaze. The two geldings stopped and reared, pawing the air like fighting stallions. Blaze nipped at Domino's legs and the black leaped in the air and kicked out. Cricket ran in half circles, looking back inquisitively. Then the two geldings ran side by side, full tilt down the pasture. They gathered speed and as they neared the gate they both broke stride for an instant. With a tremendous leap Domino cleared the top rail and Blaze followed after. The two horses raced down the driveway. They turned out of the driveway in a bound and thundered down the street. Cricket neighed shrilly and ran up and down the fence in a panic at being left behind.

"Oh, dear, we've got to catch them," Miss Butterfield cried. "They could get hit by a car or fall on the pavement. Get a lead rope." She ran to her car.

Uncle Tom hurried to the pickup truck and started the

motor. "Denny, get on Cricket and see if you can track them. I'll try to see where they're going."

"Come on, Claudia, we'll follow in my car." Miss Butterfield ran to her coupé and opened the door. Claudia started after her, hesitated, and ran to the stable and came back with two lead ropes. She slammed the door and they roared down the driveway. As they turned down the street Claudia put a restraining hand on Miss Butterfield's arm. "There's Mom!" Miss Butterfield put on the brakes and they jerked to a stop. "Blaze and Domino jumped the fence!" Claudia leaned from the window gesturing wildly. "Denny's on Cricket and Uncle Tom is in his pickup truck." Miss Butterfield threw the car in gear, and they raced down the street. Mary Wolff stood for a moment and then hurried toward the house.

An hour later the two cars drove into the lane and slowly came to a stop. Uncle Tom stepped out of the pickup truck and stared at Denny and his mother sitting on the doorstep. Miss Butterfield climbed out, her shoulders drooping, and Claudia, her face tear-stained, followed slowly.

"We couldn't find Blaze," Claudia said. "I didn't think he'd ever run away."

"Did you see them, Denny?" Uncle Tom asked.

"I didn't but Mom did." Denny grinned mischievously.

"Oh, my beautiful Domino." Miss Butterfield wiped her eyes, holding her glasses, as she dabbed with a wisp of a handkerchief. "If anything happens to him I shall never forgive myself for turning him into the pasture." She looked at Denny. "What is so amusing?"

"Well, where did your mother see them, Denny?" Uncle Tom said quickly.

"In the stable!" Denny chuckled and his mother smiled at the trio of worried faces.

"I hadn't been home two minutes until Blaze came running back with Domino at his heels. I just opened the gate and they went right in," their mother said. "They're both in Domino's stall munching hay." She put an arm around Claudia's shoulders. "They must have just circled around."

"I was so worried about Domino I didn't think about Blaze coming home," Uncle Tom said. "All I could think of was Domino being in a strange place and that he'd go back to his former home."

"Well, I guess Blaze just told him he lives here now," Claudia murmured.

"We won't turn them out in the pasture again," Miss Butterfield said with relief.

"Of course we can." Uncle Tom grinned and shifted his foot as he reached for his pipe. "Only this time we'll turn them out one at a time until they get over their playing." He tapped the tobacco in the bowl firmly. "I don't suppose Domino has had that much freedom in his whole life."

"It must be terrible for a horse to have to live in a box stall all his life," their mother said.

"Yes," Uncle Tom said, "it's natural for horses to live in the open. If you give them a choice you'll find that the only thing that drives them to shelter is wind."

"Well," Miss Butterfield sighed, "I've had enough excitement for one day." She pushed her shirt firmly into

84

the belt of her riding pants. "I think I'll go home. If you think you should put the chain on Domino for the night you go right ahead," she said to Uncle Tom.

"I think we'd better for a few days," he told her. "I'll take care of it." They watched her climb back into her car and drive out of the yard. "We'd better check Blaze and Domino to see if they're hot," he said to the children. "We may have to walk them out. Don't want them catching cold."

Uncle Tom and Denny got lead ropes and brought Blaze and Domino out. Both animals were wet with sweat about the shoulders and flanks. Denny laid his hand on Blaze's shoulder. "He's a little warm . . . I'd better cool him a little." Claudia and her mother sat watching them.

Claudia stoop up, sighed, and walked over to watch Uncle Tom and Denny replace the collar and chain on Domino's leg.

"I'll walk him," she offered.

"He's still warm," Uncle Tom said. "It will do him good to make him walk. It will remind him not to kick."

"I guess we'd better get the boards to finish the stalls tomorrow," Denny said.

"I'll pick them up for you if you want," Uncle Tom offered.

"We'd better wait a while," Claudia spoke up. Denny stared at her and then smiled across at Uncle Tom.

"I'll never figure Claudia out." His eyes probed hers. "She's up to something again. Just the other day she wanted the stalls up right away." He followed Uncle Tom out of the corral. Uncle Tom fastened the gate and they walked slowly to the house.

"You don't want Domino to kick down a brand-new stall, do you?" Claudia called after them.

"All right, as soon as he's trained you let us know," Denny threw over his shoulder. "Gosh, I'm hungry."

"So am I," Uncle Tom said. "This has been another one of those days."

When they reached the kitchen door the odor of pot roast filled their nostrils.

"Oh, Denny, Mr. Kendall called and wants you to come down to the stable tomorrow after school." His mother studied his face. "He says he has something to say to you."

Denny stood for a moment and then pulled out a chair and sat studying his plate. A worried frown creased his forehead.

"I guess he has another trail ride for Saturday," Claudia said brightly.

"Oh, no, he hasn't," Denny spoke quickly.

"Well, how much did you make on the last one?" Claudia asked.

"Not much, only three dollars," Denny admitted.

"That's all right," Uncle Tom commented. He smiled across at their mother and then sobered as she shook her head slightly at him. His eyes probed Denny's face and then he attacked his supper with relish.

"You know," Claudia mused, "everything really turns out all right." She looked around the table. "Domino got loose today but Blaze brought him back. You see?"

"Yes, Claudia, we see." Her mother smiled at her gently.

"Well, that was just luck," Denny retorted.

"No, it wasn't," Claudia argued. The telephone rang.

"Children, children, let's not make an issue of it. Just be glad the horses got back safely," their mother corrected. She picked up the receiver. Claudia wrinkled her nose at Denny. He sat back and grinned at her and then turned his attention to his mother and listened to her conversation.

"Yes, Mr. Davis, tomorrow then." Their mother put the receiver down.

"Who was that?" Denny wanted to know.

"That was Mr. Davis, the real-estate man." Their mother watched their faces. "He has a lady who is interested in buying the ranch."

8. THE JOB

CLAUDIA was sitting on the back doorstep when the long, black automobile belonging to Mr. Davis turned into the driveway and stopped with a cloud of dust. A gray-haired man in a business suit opened the car door and helped a tall, well-dressed woman out of the car. She scanned the stableyard and critically studied the house and then turned an indifferent gaze on Claudia. Mary Wolff came to the door and greeted them with a smile.

"This is the lady I called you about, Mrs. Wolff," Mr. Davis said. "Mrs. Holcomb, Mrs. Wolff." Claudia stood up, her face drained white, and she eyed the woman with suspicion. "Mrs. Holcomb'd like to look about," Mr. Davis said.

"Of course, just show her around, Mr. Davis." Mary Wolff opened the door for them and then went to the kitchen and started washing the dishes.

"You can look at the house first," Mr. Davis offered. "Then I'll show you the grounds. It's equipped for horses, you know." Mrs. Holcomb followed him to the living room and Claudia eased along behind them. "This is a very comfortable house, as you can see."

"This might do." Mrs. Holcomb followed him to the hallway and peeked into the bedrooms. "I guess it could be converted into a chicken ranch easily enough."

Claudia gasped and Mrs. Holcomb turned to look at her. Claudia moved around in front of Mr. Davis. "We're going to a nicer place," she put in. "This one needs a lot of repairing." Mr. Davis glared down at Claudia. Taking Mrs. Holcomb by the arm, he tried to hurry her along.

Claudia shot a swift glance toward the kitchen but her mother, Denny, and Uncle Tom were busily talking. "If the highway comes through here, will they have to move this house?" Claudia's expressive face was all innocence.

"You didn't say anything about a highway." Mrs. Holcomb faced the real-estate dealer with suspicion. She regarded Claudia for a moment and then turned and walked to the back door without speaking. She went directly to the car and climbed in and sat down. Mr. Davis reached Mary Wolff's side almost as soon as Claudia did. He frowned at Claudia as she slid an arm around her mother's waist and held her tight.

"Mrs. Wolff," he said crisply, "I cannot sell real estate if your daughter is going to discredit the property." He turned on his heel and strode to the car. They watched him wheel the car out the driveway.

"Claudia, what did you do?" Her mother's voice was stern.

"Well, I just asked him if the highway was coming through this property," she said calmly. "I heard you and Uncle Tom talking about it," she finished lamely.

"It's going through a half mile from here," her mother said.

"I know that, but I just asked," Claudia said stubbornly.

"Claudia, you know we have to sell," her mother said quietly. "You can't discourage prospective buyers."

"We could wait a while," Claudia pleaded. "We've already got one boarder. If we had another ..."

"That isn't enough," her mother told her.

"We'll never get enough boarders to save the ranch," Denny put in.

"How do you know?" Claudia flung at him. "We could wait another month." Claudia pulled at her mother's arm. "We could give you the forty dollars Miss Butterfield paid us. We don't have to finish Blaze's and Cricket's stalls right away." Her mother smoothed the brown hair from the clear forehead. "Honest, Mom, if you'll just wait ..."

"Claudia." Her mother cupped her chin in her hands. "You're such a manager."

"Then you will?" Claudia smiled with her eyes.

"No, Claudia," her mother said. "We have to sell when we can. Now let's clear things up here in the kitchen."

Claudia looked down at her hands and sighed deeply. Uncle Tom patted her on the shoulder. Finally she shrugged her shoulders. "Well, anyway, I'm going to ride Cricket tomorrow."

Miss Butterfield was saddling Domino when Claudia and Dennis came home from school. She had just put on the bridle when Denny came out of the house dressed in a clean Western shirt and jeans. Claudia changed into an old, faded pair of jeans and rushed to the stable, pushing her mussed hair back into her pony tail.

"My, don't you look nice," Miss Butterfield said, looking at Denny. Claudia came walking back. She giggled and Denny scowled at her.

"I'm going down to Kendall's," Denny said.

"Could you help me tie this ribbon on Domino's tail?" Miss Butterfield pulled a length of red ribbon from her pocket.

"I have to go to the stables right away," Denny said, opening the gate to Blaze's stall. "Mr. Kendall just phoned again. He wants to see me."

"It will only take a moment if you'll hold Domino," she begged.

"He might get his shirt dirty." Claudia chuckled. "Why don't you tie the ribbon to his mane? Domino will look prettier."

"It isn't for decoration," Miss Butterfield said bluntly.

90

"But ... to his tail!" Claudia stared at her curiously.

"You always mark a kicking horse by tying a red ribbon to his tail," Miss Butterfield told her. "Denny, if you will back him up to the fence I can reach over and tie the ribbon."

"He doesn't even try to kick with the chain on," Claudia said, watching Denny lead Domino into the paddock. Miss Butterfield waited until he had backed Domino up to the fence and then she reached over and tied the ribbon to the hair at the top of his tail.

Denny hurriedly saddled Blaze and cantered out of the yard. Miss Butterfield and Claudia followed at a slower pace. Claudia walked Cricket along the edge of the road. She watched Cricket's head bob and didn't talk. Miss Butterfield glanced at her frequently but Claudia appeared deep in thought. Finally she pulled Domino to a stop. Claudia, startled out of her reverie, reined Cricket and turned to Miss Butterfield with surprise.

"Do you feel all right?" Miss Butterfield asked, observing her closely.

"I feel all right," Claudia said and started Cricket in a walk again.

"Don't you want to talk? Are you angry with me ... because Domino ran away yesterday?" Miss Butterfield asked anxiously.

"Oh no," Claudia said. "I like you, Miss Butterfield." She grew quiet for a moment. "Well, you see ..." she began, "Denny and I want to have a real stable so we can help Mom and Dad keep the ranch. We saved to buy Blaze and built the stable. Now we should have at least two more boarders before we have a real stable."

"Well, I shall certainly tell my friends," she said. "Miss Brown is getting a horse, you know."

"How soon?" Claudia asked eagerly.

"As soon as she finds exactly what she wants," Miss Butterfield answered.

"Oh." Claudia bit her lip with disappointment. She trotted ahead as they reached the lane leading down to the stableyard. Denny was leaning against the rail when she rode up. "How long have you been here?"

"About ten minutes," Denny answered. "Mr. Kendall isn't here. Why don't you go on? I'll wait."

"I just got here," Claudia answered crossly. She jumped from Cricket's back and tied her lightly. Miss Butterfield cantered Domino around the ring and Claudia watched her for a moment before she ran down the shed row to look into the stalls at the horses. Denny looked after her. Sighing, he turned and leaned backward against Blaze. He dug his heel into the soft dirt and glanced frequently up the lane. When he saw Sam Kendall drive in, he straightened and waited.

Sam Kendall nodded when he saw him. After parking his car, he hurried over and gave Blaze a slap on the rump. "I'm glad you came, Denny." He thrust his chin out and flexed his heavy arms as he hooked his thumbs over his belt. "I owe you an apology." He hesitated. Denny waited, watching his face. "Freddie told me what happened on the trail ... when I got around to listening to him. I should have known. Clift has upset things around here before." He put a hand on Denny's shoulder. "Well, am I forgiven?"

"Sure, Mr. Kendall." Denny grinned.

"I could use you for a week," Sam Kendall began. "My man is sick again. I'd like you to take the trail rides out Saturday and Sunday also."

"Thanks, Mr. Kendall," Denny said happily. "I'll sure be glad to."

"You come down after school," Sam Kendall directed. "I've decided to work you in as relief around here." He stood with his hands on his hips watching the horses in the ring. "I see Miss Butterfield is riding Domino."

93

"Yeah, Uncle Tom is helping her with him," Denny said. They watched Miss Butterfield put Domino through his paces. A low sports car rolled down the lane and came to a stop before Sam and Denny. A short, stout, white-haired man pulled himself up and out of the car and strode toward Sam with his hand out.

"Sam, my boy," he bellowed jovially, "it's been a long time."

"Jonas Pomeroy!" Sam shouted. "How're the Pomeroy enterprises and those fast thoroughbreds?"

"Great, great. Two fifty-thousand-dollar handicaps." Jonas Pomeroy slapped Sam on the shoulder and shadow-boxed a little. "You have a nice place here." Jonas looked around and then smiled at Denny. "Is this one of your young men?"

"This is Dennis Wolff," Sam said. "He helps me when I need someone." Denny grinned at the little man with the happy countenance and held out his hand. Jonas pumped it vigorously. "He has his own horse."

"Always like young people. You'll have to come out and see my ranch." He put his pudgy hands on his hips and watched Miss Butterfield work Domino. "Now there's a likely thoroughbred." He scanned the shed row and his glance rested for a brief moment on Cricket and then he walked over to her. He sobered and was serious as he studied her face and walked around her. "Where did this little pony come from, Sam? Looks like a Welsh. I've seen her before."

"Oh, some old man brought her in here to sell. Denny's sister bought her for five dollars." Sam chuckled.

"What was the man's name?" Jonas Pomeroy held

Cricket's muzzle in his hand and studied her face. "Looks like one of my own ponies."

"It said Binder on the receipt," Denny spoke up.

"Binder!" Jonas Pomeroy turned on his heel. "I sold a weanling Welsh filly to Eddie Binder about four years ago." He nodded his head. "You know, I think this is the filly."

"She's just a skinny little horse as far as I'm concerned," Sam Kendall retorted. "She looks better now than when Claudia bought her, though."

"You say she paid five dollars for this filly." Jonas dropped his hands to his sides and stared at Sam. "Five dollars! This is the only daughter of my Revel Time, one of the finest Welsh stallions to come out of Wales!"

"Gee!" Denny regarded Jonas Pomeroy. His eyes lit with excitement. "Wait until Claudia hears this." Denny ran down the shed row shouting for Claudia. At the back of the barn, when he called again, she stuck her head out of a manger.

"Here I am. I was feeding this Arabian." She grinned up at him as she pushed another handful of hay into the eager mouth of the dappled gray horse.

"Come on, Claudia, there's a man here who knows Cricket." He grasped her hand and pulled her along. "She's purebred Welsh."

Claudia stopped and pulled back. She stood looking at him, disbelief in her eyes. Then the realization of what Denny said became clear and her face wreathed itself in a bright smile. "Uncle Tom said she was well bred." Claudia ran ahead of him and rushed up to Cricket. She threw her arms around Cricket's neck and hugged her close. "You said she wasn't any good." She pouted at Sam Kendall. Her eyes probed Jonas Pomeroy. "Is she really a Welsh pony?"

"She's bred from one of the best pony lines there is," Jonas Pomeroy told her. "I remember her, now, as a weanling."

"What is a Welsh pony?" Claudia wanted to know. "I thought ponies were ponies."

"Oh, no," Jonas Pomeroy explained. "There are many breeds of ponies. The Welsh is one of the prettiest. They look like a miniature horse."

"If she's the only daughter of Revel Time, why did you sell her?" Sam looked puzzled.

"Well, I had to take some horses to the race track and I told my wife she could sell one of the two fillies in the back pasture. To make a long story short, my wife sold the wrong one, made out the papers and all. I tried to buy her back but the young fellow wouldn't sell." He turned to Claudia. "Did you get the papers on this filly?"

"Of course she didn't," Sam put in. "We had no idea. This old man brought her down here and tried to sell her to me."

"Old man! She was sold to a young man." Jonas fingered his chin. "You'd have to have a transfer of sale before you can get her registration cleared for ownership." Jonas studied Claudia's sober face. "Would you like to sell her?"

"Oh, I couldn't!" Claudia held tightly to the little mare.

"I'll give you a thousand dollars for her just as she is."

Jonas Pomeroy waited for an answer. Claudia faced him stiffly and her glance flicked to Denny.

"Gee, Claudia, that would save the ranch." Denny's eyes were bright. Claudia buried her face in Cricket's mane. Her arms tightened around the brown neck. Finally she turned around but she didn't speak. Denny shifted impatiently. "What do you say, Claudia?"

"I have Binder's address," Jonas Pomeroy went on. "I'll go see him as soon as I leave here. We'll get this all straightened out. I'd like to get a colt out of Cricket; best line there is."

"But the boy is in the service," Sam reminded him.

"Well, he lived with his uncle, he should know about it," Jonas said. "He probably signed the transfer before he left." Claudia turned her back to them and put her face against Cricket's soft muzzle.

Denny looked at her for a moment and then turned to Mr. Pomeroy. "How does it happen she's the only daughter of Revel Time?" he wanted to know.

"Revel Time died of colic," Jonas Pomeroy explained. "I have one of his sons as a junior herd sire and my senior herd sire is now Red Quill."

"Well, then," Denny went on, "a colt out of Cricket would be worth a lot of money."

"That's right," Jonas Pomeroy said. "Claudia is fortunate to have Cricket."

"Yeah," Denny said happily. "Did you want me to start working today?" He grinned at Sam Kendall.

"No," Sam told him. "I want to visit with Jonas. Go ahead and work your horse and I'll discuss it with you later."

97

"Come on, Claudia, let's ride around the ring," Denny suggested. "Isn't it swell about Cricket?"

"I don't want to ride." Claudia hung back and stood close to Cricket. Denny frowned at her, hesitated, and then shrugged his shoulders. He mounted Blaze and sat looking at Cricket with speculation; and then smiled to himself. He began to work Blaze along with Miss Butterfield and Domino. The two horses paced each other around the ring. Jonas Pomeroy watched them as he stood talking to Sam. He walked through the stables with Sam and then came back to stand and watch Denny again. Finally Sam called, "Denny, come over here a moment."

Denny turned Blaze easily and came to a smooth stop. "Jonas was wondering if you'd like to go out to the track and exercise thoroughbreds." Denny glanced from Sam Kendall to Jonas Pomeroy with surprise. He jumped down and his face was bright with excitement.

"I sort of promised Mr. Kendall, sir," Denny began seriously.

"It would mean getting up early on Saturday mornings," Sam told him. "It would take you about two hours at the track and then you could come here to the stable by noon and take my trail rides out."

"That would be great." Denny was pleased. "I think I should talk it over with my mother, though, before I say yes."

"That's what I like to hear." Jonas Pomeroy clapped Denny on the shoulder. "Suppose I come meet your mother and talk to her myself?"

"That would be fine." Denny smiled at him.

"I'll see you this evening then," Jonas Pomeroy said.

"I'll find this Binder fellow. We'll wrap everything up this evening." He climbed into his car and sped out of the stableyard. Sam watched him go and then began to talk to Denny.

Denny listened closely as Sam pointed out the different horses he would be caring for. "I'll give you a list of the ones I want grained. You can feed them after school and clean whatever stalls need it. I'll pay you by the hour, shouldn't take you more than a couple of hours to do this work every afternoon."

"I can do that all right, Mr. Kendall," Denny assured him. "I'll be down tomorrow afternoon to start then." Sam nodded. "I guess we'd better go. I want to tell my Mom about Mr. Pomeroy."

"I'll be right with you." Miss Butterfield brought Domino to a halt beside Mr. Kendall. "Now what do you think of Domino?" She smiled down at Sam.

"I always liked him," Sam explained. "But I have no time for a kicking horse." He ran his hand down Domino's flank. The black put his ears back and raised a leg menacingly. Miss Butterfield slapped him smartly on the neck and he put his foot down again. Sam grinned. "I guess he's learning."

Denny looked for Claudia. The space where she had stood with Cricket was bare. He tied Blaze and walked the length of the shed row. He came back. "Have you seen Claudia?"

"No," they both answered. Denny was quiet and a frown creased his forehead as he slowly untied Blaze and pulled himself into the saddle.

9. THE NEW OWNER

DENNY and Miss Butterfield trotted their horses briskly down the road. There was a perplexed expression on Denny's face.

"I never thought things would turn out this way." Denny was excited. "I have a job with Mr. Kendall and maybe one with Mr. Pomeroy and then Claudia's pony is worth so much. We'll be able to work everything out." He looked back. "I wonder where Claudia is?" He glanced at Miss Butterfield. "I wish Claudia could keep Cricket, though. Of course she can ride Blaze as she did before."

"Maybe she won't want to sell her," Miss Butterfield said. "Sometimes there are things more important than money."

"Oh, she wasn't going to be able to keep her anyway," Denny said quickly. "She bought her with the grocery money when she wasn't supposed to," Denny explained. "She didn't even ask me." Denny looked thoughtful. "Of course, when a horse is worth that much it's foolish not to sell it."

"Would you sell Blaze?" Miss Butterfield gave him a quizzical glance.

"Oh, that's different," Denny said. "We saved a long time for him and we both bought him with the money we saved."

"Yes, it is different," Miss Butterfield agreed. "You remember my friend, Miss Brown? She was with me when I bought Domino. She has found a horse she wants. She looked a long time." Miss Butterfield eyed him. "Now that she's found it she would never want to sell."

"But Claudia bought this pony because she felt sorry for it," Denny protested.

"But there is something about a horse that gets under your skin," Miss Butterfield said quietly. "You know how you feel about Blaze. Claudia must feel the same way about Cricket."

"But she's always known that she might have to give her up." Denny turned, giving her his full back as he dug a heel into Blaze's side and raced toward the driveway. He gave a quick look at the Flying W sign and turned in between the two posts without slowing down.

"Mom, Mom!" he shouted. His mother hurried out the back door, wiping her hands on her apron. Her smooth face had a look of concern until she saw Denny's smile. She pushed a wisp of hair back from her face and secured it with a hairpin. Denny flung himself out of the saddle and rushed up to her. "Cricket's a purebred! She's worth a thousand dollars!" He caught his breath and then explained what had happened at the stable.

"I can't believe it," his mother said. "Why would that man sell her to Claudia for five dollars?" She glanced around. "Where's Claudia?"

"Isn't she here?" Denny's face sobered. "She left the stable before we did. I thought she came home."

"I haven't seen her." His mother's forehead creased with worry. She walked to the stable. "Cricket isn't here either." She was thoughtful. "Where could she be? We have to find her before she does something foolish."

"What could she do?" Denny wanted to know.

"Claudia just won't admit failure," his mother said. "She might think of hiding Cricket somewhere. She'll try to solve this problem in her own way." Denny tied Blaze and then walked over beside his mother.

"Isn't it thrilling news?" Miss Butterfield trotted Domino to the stable and climbed down. She began to loosen the cinch. "It's exciting to discover you have a really good horse." She patted Domino's sleek neck, pulled the saddle off, and turned him into the paddock. She hung the bridle on the rack and put her saddle away. "By the way, Alice Brown will probably be calling you about boarding her horse." Denny gave a fleeting smile in her direction and nodded. But when he faced his mother he sobered at her unsmiling face. "I'll see you tomorrow," Miss Butterfield called over her shoulder and walked to her car. His mother gave her a slight wave and then turned toward the stable. She stood looking into Cricket's stall and then let her glance flick about the corral and the pasture.

"Maybe she didn't come home," Denny said grimly.

"This isn't like Claudia, not to tell me what she's going to do." His mother faced around. "Even if she hid the pony she'd tell me."

"Maybe she wouldn't," Denny said.

"Oh, yes. She might not tell me where but she'd tell me what she'd done." She hesitated. "What did Claudia say when she found out about Cricket?"

"She didn't say anything," Denny said. "After Mr. Pomeroy wanted to buy Cricket she didn't do or say anything. I thought she'd be glad. It means we can save the ranch." He tried again. "It isn't as if she'd had Cricket the way we've had Blaze."

"You must remember that, deep down, Claudia has wanted a horse of her own," his mother told him.

"But she knew we couldn't afford it," Denny insisted.

"Where would she go?" his mother said anxiously.

"I'm going to call Uncle Tom," Denny said and ran to the house. His mother walked to the pasture fence and, putting her hands on the top rail, began to scan the pasture area closely. She was still standing by the fence when Denny came out of the house.

"Isn't that a horse down by the tree at the corner of the pasture?" She pointed and Denny could see the switch of a tail from behind the walnut tree that stood on the property line. "Go over there and see, Denny."

Denny started running across the pasture. His mother followed. Claudia was sitting under the walnut tree, her elbows on her knees and her face cupped in her hands. She looked up at Denny, then got to her feet.

"What are you doing down here?" Denny cried. Her face was tear-stained and she hurriedly wiped her hands across her cheeks when she saw her mother coming.

"I just wanted to think," Claudia said quickly.

"Claudia!" her mother called. "Why didn't you stop at the house? I was worried about you." Claudia stood silent. She eyed them both sullenly.

"I told Mom about Cricket," Denny admitted.

"Oh," was all Claudia could say.

103

"So Mr. Pomeroy offered you a thousand dollars," her mother began. "It just doesn't seem possible."

"That would just about save the ranch, wouldn't it, Mom?" Denny didn't look at Claudia.

"It would make a difference indeed," his mother admitted.

"Oh, Mom!" Claudia burst into tears and threw her arms around her mother. Her mother brushed the smooth brown hair and, taking a corner of her apron, wiped the tears from her face. Claudia sniffled, swallowed, and straightened up.

"Let's go to the house," her mother said quietly.

"I'll bring Cricket," Denny offered. He picked up the reins and then called to them, "Say, you should be careful, Claudia, there's a lot of barbed wire in this corner. Cricket might have got tangled up in it."

"I saw it but I was watching her," Claudia said. "I want to take Cricket myself." She took the reins from Denny and walked slowly toward the corral.

As they neared the house they heard the truck drive into the yard. It rambled to a stop with a familiar unpainted horse trailer bumping along behind. When a thin, unkempt figure climbed out, Claudia took hold of Denny's arm. "It's that Mr. Binder," she whispered.

"I had a time finding where you lived," Mr. Binder greeted them harshly. "I've come to buy the mare back." He eyed their mother watchfully and turned his attention to Claudia. "I'll give you your five dollars back."

"I should say not." Denny gave a short laugh and shifted his weight as he grinned across at his mother.

"I'm afraid you've made a mistake..." their mother began.

"All right, all right, I'll make it ten." Mr. Binder hooked a thumb under his suspender and walked impatiently back and forth in front of them.

"I can't sell her to you at all, now," Claudia said quickly.

"You can't keep her," Mr. Binder said angrily.

"I know," Claudia murmured and studied the reins in her hands.

"You haven't got the papers," Mr. Binder went on. He pulled a yellow paper from his back pocket. "She's no good to you without these. This is her pedigree." He waved the paper under their noses and continued to talk. "You should be glad for me to take her off your hands." He shoved the paper back into his pocket. "You'd better let me have her before I change my mind. I got no time to fool around waiting for you to make up your mind. If you don't..." He suddenly stopped talking as Uncle Tom's pickup truck pulled into the yard. Claudia ran to him. He put an arm around her shoulders and studied her pale face.

"Are you all right? You weren't lost?" He held her chin in his hand.

"He's trying to take Cricket back," Claudia told him.

"What!" Uncle Tom frowned across at Mr. Binder. "What's this nonsense?"

"I'm willing to take that mare off her hands." Mr. Binder thrust his chin out. "I'll give you twenty-five dollars for her. That's my final price." He pulled out a soiled wallet and opened it. But before Uncle Tom could

105

speak the low sports car of Jonas Pomeroy wheeled into the yard and came to a dusty stop under the pepper tree. Jonas Pomeroy puffed as he pulled himself out of the car. A young man in Navy blues followed him. He shoved the white hat back on his brown crew cut and stopped to brush the lint from his blouse. He ran a finger over the three white stripes that indicated his rank and straightened up to face Mr. Binder.

"What are you doin' here, Eddie?" Mr. Binder gave the young sailor a scowling look.

"I got four days' leave." Eddie put his hands on his hips. "When I got to your house, Mr. Pomeroy was there. He told me you'd sold my pony. What's the idea?"

"Don't tell me what to do," Mr. Binder shouted. "You didn't tell me what this pony was worth."

"You said you'd keep her for me," Eddie shouted back.

"You thought you could get her back and then sell her to me for a big price," Jonas Pomeroy put in. "I should have known better than to tell you over the telephone." He turned to Eddie. "You didn't sign a transfer of ownership?"

"I didn't sign anything," Eddie said. "He promised to keep her for me until I got out of the service."

"He didn't have any right to sell her," Jonas Pomeroy said.

"I sold her because I wasn't going to feed her any longer," Mr. Binder snapped.

"I sent you board money every month," Eddie insisted. "I have the receipts for my money orders."

"I have a receipt too." Claudia stepped up to Eddie. "I bought her from Mr. Binder and he gave me a receipt."

106

"So you're the little girl who bought her." Eddie studied Claudia's tear-begrimed face.

"He has Cricket's papers," Claudia told him. "Are you going to call the sheriff?"

"Better give those papers to Eddie," Jonas Pomeroy warned. Mr. Binder gave Claudia a swift glance and studied the angry faces around him. Reaching into his pocket, he pulled out the yellow sheet and thrust it into Eddie's hand.

"You'd better leave," Uncle Tom muttered and pulled at his mustache. He smoothed it quickly and adjusted his hat more firmly on his head. Mr. Binder hesitated for a moment, shrugged his shoulders, and ambled quickly toward the rickety truck. They were all quiet as they watched the trailer bump along the driveway and disappear down the road.

"Eddie, you spend your leave with me." Jonas Pomeroy put an arm across his shoulders. "I'm glad you got your pony back."

"You mean Cricket isn't mine at all?" Claudia studied their faces.

"I'm afraid that's right," Jonas Pomeroy told her.

"But I bought Cricket." Claudia drew back, blinking. "I really wanted to keep her but I was going to sell her to Mr. Pomeroy so we could stay on the ranch." Tears began to fill her eyes and she turned her back to them and looked down at her twisting fingers.

"I should have known it was too good," Denny commented grimly.

"I'm sorry." Eddie stared at Claudia's drooping shoulders. "I'll pay you for her board and give your

ERK

money back." Claudia didn't answer. "I'll find a place to keep her as soon as I can. Now, let's go see my pony."

"You mean you're going to take her away?" Claudia whirled.

"I'll have to get her settled before my leave is up," Eddie said. "I still have two years of service yet."

Denny followed Claudia and Eddie to the stable. Claudia's face was pale. Cricket stood, sleepily, near the fence. Eddie looked at her for a moment.

"She certainly doesn't look like she did when I left."

"Well," Denny defended, "she's put on some weight since Claudia bought her."

"I hope she'll be all right." Eddie sighed, put his arm around the little mare's neck, and laid his face against her cheek. Claudia lagged behind as they rejoined the group.

"It isn't fair," Claudia cried. "It just isn't fair!"

10.   WILD COW

DENNY watched Claudia's stricken face. A flush started at his collar and his eyes were bright with a growing anger.

"Claudia's done a lot for Cricket," he exploded. "She

was nothing but skin and bones when Claudia bought her. Look at her now.''

''That's right,'' her mother put in. ''Claudia has taken very good care of her.''

''Why don't you leave her here?'' Jonas Pomeroy suggested. ''As long as you must leave her someplace, this would be the best.''

''I'd want her to have the best of care,'' Eddie admitted. ''Nothing like she had at my uncle's.''

''Claudia would give her the best of care,'' Uncle Tom interrupted. ''She'd have love, too.'' Claudia gave him a grateful smile and then turned to Eddie, waiting for his answer.

''All right, I'll do it,'' Eddie said.

''Maybe you might decide to sell her someday,'' Claudia began hopefully. ''And then I could buy her.''

''You'll never have a thousand dollars,'' Denny said. The smile faded from Claudia's face.

''I forgot,'' she murmured. ''But if you ever decided to sell ...''

''I'm raising ponies as soon as I'm out of the service.'' Eddie grinned at Claudia. ''If I don't, Cricket is yours— for the price you get for the first colt. How's that?''

''You're not kidding?'' Claudia watched his face. Her eyes probed his. He shook his head slowly.

''No, I'm not kidding,'' he said. ''You've had a rough deal. I'll even put it in writing.'' Claudia turned on her heel and ran to the house. She was back in a moment with a pencil and paper.

''You really promise, cross your heart?'' She held them

110

out to him. "I have a receipt for Cricket but it isn't any good."

"This will be good," he promised her. Eddie wrote quickly, and signing his name with a flourish, he handed her the paper.

Claudia stuffed the pencil in her pocket. She smiled at Uncle Tom and read aloud. "If I do not claim Cricket in two years she will belong to Claudia Wolff for the price of her first foal."

"I'll witness it," Uncle Tom said and Claudia pulled the pencil from her pocket.

"So will I," Jonas Pomeroy said. "Maybe you and I can do some business about colts before Eddie gets back."

"I'll leave that to you," Eddie said. "I feel that she's in good hands."

"Well, now that this is settled," her mother interrupted, "why don't we all go in and have some coffee?" Claudia lagged behind, reading the words over and over again.

Denny slipped up beside her. "He'll never give Cricket up. That receipt won't do you any good either." His face was serious. "Maybe it would have been better if we hadn't asked Eddie to leave Cricket here."

"I'd rather have her just for two years than not at all," Claudia said seriously. He smiled at her and taking her arm propelled her toward the back steps.

Their mother made chocolate for Claudia and Denny and they all sat around the table talking about ponies. Jonas Pomeroy told them about his ranch, his herd of Welsh ponies, and his racing thoroughbreds.

"I've asked Denny to come out for a trial exercising

111

thoroughbreds,'' Jonas Pomeroy said to their mother. ''I think Denny has the hands of a trainer. That's something hard to find.''

''Well, I don't know.'' His mother faced Uncle Tom. ''I think you know what Denny is capable of better than I.'' She smiled at Denny. ''I want him to have every opportunity to do what he wants.''

''It will be good experience for him,'' Uncle Tom agreed.

''Then how about coming out to the ranch in the morning and you can put a saddle on one of them,'' Jonas Pomeroy suggested. ''We'll try you out.'' He looked around at the rest of them, then smiled at Claudia. ''There are some fine wild blackberries down by the creek, perhaps you would like to pick some.''

''Oh, may we?'' Claudia smiled anxiously at her mother.

''If Uncle Tom will drive us out.'' Her mother faced Uncle Tom and he nodded.

''Could we take Cricket, too?'' Claudia asked.

''Oh, no, dear,'' her mother protested. ''We couldn't do that.''

''But Cricket might like to visit her old home again,'' Claudia insisted.

''Now, that's a good idea,'' Jonas Pomeroy said. ''I'll call Sam Kendall and you can go by and pick up a trailer.''

''I'll have to be back by noon to work for Mr. Kendall.'' Denny glanced at Claudia and then at his mother.

''That's right.'' His mother chuckled. ''My, so much is happening, I can't keep up with it.''

"Would you like to ride, too, Eddie?" Jonas Pomeroy asked the sailor.

"I want to see my girl tomorrow," Eddie replied. "But I'm taking you up on staying with you for the balance of my leave."

"Right." Jonas Pomeroy nodded.

"Thanks, Mr. Pomeroy, I think I made some real friends today." Eddie smiled across at Claudia. "I guess things turned out pretty well for you, after all."

"I can hardly wait until tomorrow," Claudia said.

It was right after breakfast that Uncle Tom drove Claudia and her mother out to the Pomeroy ranch. Jonas Pomeroy came in after Denny and led the way in the sports car. The Pomeroy ranch nestled at the base of the hills about a mile beyond the Kendall stables. From the porch of the low ranch house the great split in the rock of the Lost Hills Canyon looked like the large eye of a needle. The rambling white stables looked as if they were braced by the many square paddocks. The long pastures rolled like green carpets, fanning away from the main group of buildings while the exercise ring in front of the main stable was the hub of the whole ranch. Jonas Pomeroy stopped his car in the small parking lot near the main barn and Uncle Tom pulled the pickup truck and trailer alongside. Denny jumped out and went to watch a trainer lead a yearling around on a longe line, trying to teach the youngster to circle around him.

"This is a real ranch," Claudia cried when she reached Denny's side. Uncle Tom put the tail gate down and backed Cricket out of the trailer. Claudia skipped over beside Jonas Pomeroy. "Is this really where Cricket used to live?"

"She was foaled in that pasture back of the house," Jonas Pomeroy told her. "Come along and I'll show you around." He turned to Uncle Tom. "You can tie Cricket near the door to that hitching ring until you've seen the barns." He glanced toward the house. "I wish my wife were here today. She had to run into town. She would have liked to meet all of you."

Jonas Pomeroy led them down the long, cool, clean interior of the main barn. Stalls lined the sides and the horses came to the doors and hung their heads over the edges to look and smell.

"Are all these race horses?" Claudia asked, stopping to rub the velvet nose of a smooth bay who nickered at her touch.

"They're all thoroughbreds, which, of course, means they are all racing animals," Jonas Pomeroy explained. "I have a few training at the track." He stopped at a large roomy stall and called to the big chestnut, who came at once to the door. "This is my thoroughbred sire, Pomeroy's Pride. Some of these others are promising youngsters. The mares are out in the pastures and also this year's crop of foals."

"Where are the ponies?" Claudia wanted to know. "Where's Red Quill?"

"In the next barn, the smaller one." Jonas Pomeroy led the way out to the shed row.

"It must be swell to work with these purebred horses," Denny said quietly.

"Well," Jonas Pomeroy smiled at him, "if you are as

114

good a horseman as Sam Kendall says you are maybe you'll be working for me this summer.''

"Did Mr. Kendall say that?" Denny asked.

"He did indeed," Jonas Pomeroy assured him. "But don't let him know I told you. He likes to act tough with boys, thinks he might spoil them if he doesn't." He chuckled. "And now for the Welsh ponies."

Jonas Pomeroy took a leather lead strap from a hook beside a stall. Opening the door, he went inside and returned leading a red Welsh stallion. The pony tossed his head and danced, as if on springs. He carried his tail high and arched his neck so that the flaxen mane tossed like silk tassels in the wind. "This is Red Quill."

"He's beautiful," Claudia said admiringly. "Of course I think Cricket is a pretty bay, though."

"Her dam was black," Jonas Pomeroy explained. "You can't always count on the color you want. The Welsh have every color except pinto."

"Does Cricket have a fancy name?" Claudia asked.

"Revel's Duchess," Jonas Pomeroy told her.

"That's quite a name," Uncle Tom said. "What value is Red Quill?"

"He's worth seven thousand dollars," Jonas Pomeroy said. "He is the only son of Revel Time. That is why I was glad to find Cricket. I didn't want his line to die out."

"What would Cricket be worth?" Claudia looked at Red Quill with awe, her eyes wide with excitement.

"When she was a yearling I wouldn't have taken eight hundred dollars for her," Jonas Pomeroy said solemnly.

"Eight hundred dollars!" Claudia stared at Jonas Pomeroy and her mouth stood open.

"You see," Uncle Tom chided her. "You see what a good buy you made for five dollars."

"But why didn't Mr. Binder try to sell her for more?" Claudia finally said when she was able to talk. "Didn't he know what she was worth?"

"He let her get terribly thin," Uncle Tom said. "I doubt that he knew she had papers until Mr. Pomeroy called him on the telephone and began to ask questions."

"He wasn't even going to talk to me." Jonas Pomeroy chuckled. "He thought I wanted to make him take the mare back," he explained. "Then when I mentioned the papers he suddenly became interested and said he'd look right into it. He probably went through his nephew's things and found the pedigree papers."

"Well, I'm glad Cricket has a royal name," Claudia said, and her eyes were deeply blue with thought. "I'd like her anyhow, even if she wasn't anything special." They walked up and down the shed rows looking at ponies.

"How many acres do you have?" Uncle Tom looked out over the rolling pastures of the ranch.

"About five hundred acres," Jonas Pomeroy explained. "Probably a hundred acres of pasture. Some of the land runs back toward the canyon. Some of it I haven't seen for a long time." They walked back toward the main barn. "I've got two dry milk cows back in one pasture that I haven't seen for a month. I told my foreman he'd better have a look at them. We should be having calves any day now." He turned to Claudia and her mother. "Why don't you and Claudia take your buckets and pick some blackberries while I explain to Uncle Tom and Denny how I run the thoroughbred end of my ranch? I'll have him try his

hand at handling one of my horses while you're gone."
Claudia ran to where Cricket was tied. She threw her
arms around the mare's neck and hugged her tightly.

"You'd better take good care of your pony," her
mother told her.

"I'll watch her," Claudia promised. "May I ride her
down to the berry patch?"

"Of course," Jonas Pomeroy said. "Just keep on this
side. The berries grow right along the edge of the water.
The land rolls away from a bluff. You'll see the bushes as
you top the hill, they're about five feet beyond the bluff."
He pointed to a line of Lombardy poplars. "Just this side
of the poplars is a crossfence, you can't miss it." Claudia's mother took the buckets out of the pickup truck and
waited for Claudia to mount Cricket.

Claudia adjusted the Indian bridle. "Someday you'll
have the most beautiful bridle in the world," she told
Cricket, stroking the pony's nose. She jumped easily on
the round back. The pony's body was beginning to show
a compactness that resembled Red Quill's. Claudia rode
slowly beside her mother and they stopped frequently to
look toward the herd of Welsh ponies feeding at the top
of the hill.

When they reached the last rise they saw the tops of
the blackberry bushes peeking above the shallow bluff.
They found the path leading down the bluff and saw the
blackberry bushes sprawling along the banks of the creek,
sending long streamers down into the shallow water. The
creek was wide but only ankle-deep. It looked like a trans-
parent veil fluttering over the round rocks on the bottom.
There were many narrow trails down the bluffs. Across

the creek was the corner of the crossfence. As Claudia and her mother walked along the edge of the creek looking for a likely spot to pick berries, she stopped and pointed. "The fence is broken down at the corner." Her mother looked up. "We'd better tell Mr. Pomeroy when we get back."

"I wonder if any of the ponies got out?" Her mother looked around at the empty pasture.

"I don't think there are any horses in this pasture." Claudia slid down from Cricket's back and tied the rein around the mare's neck. The pony immediately started pulling grass and Claudia took the small bucket from her mother and began to look for berries. Claudia looked for the thickest bunches of berries and her mother stepped carefully among the streamers to avoid the thorns. Cricket stopped eating and pointed her ears at them, then she came along the path and tried to stick her nose in Claudia's bucket.

"Don't set your bucket down, Mom, Cricket will eat all your berries." Claudia giggled. "They're good, too." She thrust a few in her mouth and then looked at her stained fingers. Cricket went back to pulling at the grass in short, quick bites, following Claudia and nuzzling at the bucket. Claudia had to keep the bucket safely in front of her.

"We'll pick enough for a couple of pies and some for berries and cream," her mother said.

They picked down the line of bushes until the shiny blackberries covered the bottoms of the buckets. As they rounded one of the trampled openings to the creek bed, where only the grass survived, Claudia exclaimed, "Oh!" and stepped back quickly. Her mother hurried to her side

118

and stared in the direction of Claudia's pointed finger. A heavy spray of berry streamers made a cozy arch over a smooth patch of grass, and there, cuddled up in an awkward, bony ball, was a newborn calf.

"Look, Mom." Claudia pulled at her mother's arm. "I'll bet Mr. Pomeroy doesn't know. Maybe I should ride up and tell him."

"Perhaps you'd better," her mother agreed. "I'll wait here."

Claudia handed her partly filled bucket to her mother and boosted herself on Cricket's back. The calf raised its head, struggled to its feet, took a few wobbly steps, and bawled. The brush on their right parted and a Jersey faced them menacingly, her brown eyes angry-bright with concern for her baby. She blew noisily and shook her horns and ducked her head, licking her nose nervously. She tossed her head and trotted to the edge of the creek. Claudia's mother picked up a rock and threw it but the cow came across the creek. When the calf saw its mother it waddled toward the creek and Claudia's mother found herself in a position between the cow and the calf.

"Hurry, Mom, climb up the bluff while I hold her off," Claudia called. Kicking Cricket with her heels, she trotted down the incline. Her mother picked up a clod and threw it hard, but it broke harmlessly on the cow's solid forehead. The Jersey paused, bawled, and tossed her head menacingly at Cricket. The little mare danced nervously. Claudia's mother grasped the exposed root of a shrub that hung low on the bluff and began pulling herself up. She looked back over her shoulder.

"Claudia, be careful," her mother warned. "Remember, she's protecting her calf." The cow looked at the figure struggling up the bluff and then turned her attention to Cricket, the brown eyes flashing with anger. Claudia held her steady. The calf took a few steps toward the

bluff. The Jersey whirled toward Claudia's mother. The bank was steep and her mother clung awkwardly, trying to grasp a branch that hung over the edge. She couldn't pull herself up over the rim and was too far away from the path to scramble out of the way. The calf took a few bewildered steps toward the bluff and the cow bellowed and dashed across the creek, swinging her head close to the clinging woman, and then whirled again to face Claudia as she moved up. Cricket tried to turn toward the path.

Claudia grasped a handful of mane as Cricket shied to one side when the cow swung her head. Claudia's mother was slowly pulling herself toward the top of the bluff. Claudia urged Cricket toward the cow. Now the calf was bawling frantically, and the excited cow followed in answer, moving to join her calf one moment and deciding to fight the next. Claudia pushed Cricket forward again and the cow, in another moment of indecision, whirled and smashed against the pony's shoulder. They went down in a cloud of dust. Claudia shot over Cricket's head and landed on her shoulder. She rolled away quickly and scrambled to her feet, stumbling toward the bluff where her mother was holding fast to a root. Claudia's mother screamed when she saw Claudia stumble and fall. The calf was running on unsteady legs toward the bluff. Stumbling to her feet, the cow lowered her head and dashed for Cricket. The pony pushed herself up and, neighing angrily, rose on her hind legs and struck wildly at the cow. The cow turned as the calf came to her side and she herded it toward the water. She nosed it urgently across the shallow bed to the other side. Claudia sat down and rubbed her shoulder. Her mother let go of the root, slid down the bluff, and scrambled to Claudia's side.

"Are you hurt?" She felt of Claudia's shoulder and then looked anxiously at Cricket. The little mare stood pawing the grass and looking after the retreating cow and her calf.

"Cricket was going to kick her and I lost my balance," Claudia explained. "If I hadn't fallen off we could have chased that old cow back across the creek."

122

"She wouldn't have gone without her calf," her mother said. "You might have been hurt."

"Cricket wouldn't let her hurt me," Claudia said proudly. "Wasn't she brave?"

"Yes, she's a brave little pony to face a cow protecting her calf. Look at our berries!" Claudia climbed to her feet and walked over to pick up the bucket. The berries spread about the ground in a dark red mass.

"My bucket is still over there where you set it down." Claudia trudged over and picked it up. "There's enough here for a pie." She brushed the dirt from her jeans. "I don't want to pick any more."

"I don't think I do either." Her mother smiled. "I believe we've had enough excitement for today. Let's go back to the house."

Claudia walked over to Cricket and led her to her mother's side. "Do you want to ride back? I'll lead her," she offered.

"No indeed, you ride and I'll walk," her mother said quickly. She straightened her dress and started up the path, the buckets clanging noisily together on her arm.

When they reached the barns Jonas Pomeroy, Uncle Tom, and Denny were sitting just inside the stable door. Jonas Pomeroy held a large scrapbook on his lap and Denny was turning the pages covered with pictures of horses. He jumped to his feet when he saw Claudia and his mother.

"You should have seen me," he said excitedly. "I rode one of Mr. Pomeroy's thoroughbreds." He hurried to take the buckets from his mother's arm. He stopped when he saw the empty buckets and their dusty clothing. He looked into Claudia's face and giggled.

"We got chased by a cow who was protecting her new calf so we decided we didn't want to pick any more berries." Claudia slipped down from Cricket's back. Jonas Pomeroy closed the scrapbook and put it aside. Uncle Tom got quickly to his feet.

"Are you hurt?" Jonas Pomeroy looked at them with concern.

"No, we're all right," Claudia's mother assured him. "But you have a broken fence. I guess that's how the cow got out."

"I'd better get that cow and her calf up here to the barn," Jonas Pomeroy said.

"Would you like us to help you?" Denny offered.

"No, I'll call my foreman," he said. He pulled back his sleeve and looked at his watch. "You have to be at Kendall's by noon, you won't have time. Besides, it will take some time to bring the cow up here. The calf is too young to move fast."

"You should have seen Cricket," Claudia said, rubbing Cricket's nose. "She was going to fight that cow." She turned to her mother. "Wasn't she brave?"

"Indeed," her mother agreed.

"Well," Denny interrupted, "I'm going to work my first thoroughbred on the track tomorrow morning." He grinned at Claudia. "Uncle Tom is going to drive me to the track."

"Could I go too?" Claudia begged.

"It will be early," Denny warned.

"I can get up just as early as you can," she told him.

"Isn't this exciting? Everything is happening to us."

"Nothing's dull, if that's what you mean." Uncle Tom chuckled.

"No, I mean, wonderful things are happening to us," Claudia explained.

"How can you say that after yesterday?" Denny said.

"Well..." Claudia began and then studied the ground soberly. She glanced quickly at Uncle Tom and then at her mother. "I know what you're thinking. But do we have to think of the bad things?"

11. THE RACE TRACK

CLAUDIA and Denny were up and waiting when Uncle Tom came to have breakfast with them. Denny made the toast and Claudia fried the eggs.

"We don't want to wake your mother," Uncle Tom told them as he moved around the kitchen quietly. "It's much too early for her to be up. I'll wash the dishes while you two clean the stables."

"I should do the dishes," Claudia broke in.

"I've done my share of stable cleaning." Uncle Tom

125

laughed. "Besides, you're younger than I am. I'll do the dishes." Claudia wrinkled her nose at him and grinned at Denny.

"You have to be pretty smart to out-figure Uncle Tom," Denny teased.

"Oh, I like to clean stables," Claudia said. "It's just that it's so early." They finished their breakfast and carried their dishes to the sink. Denny went outside and Claudia leaned against the sink. "Do you know where to put the dishes when you're done?"

"I'm sure I'll find the right cupboards." Uncle Tom put soap powder into the dishpan and turned on the hot water. "We'd better hurry." He turned, giving her his full back.

"Are you sure you wouldn't want me to do the dishes?" Claudia waited, then sighed and went out the back door.

Denny was raking the corral when Claudia pushed the wheelbarrow in place. She held the scoop shovel and Denny raked it full. They worked steadily until everything was clean. Denny took the scoop and rake and stood them near the stacked bails of hay. Claudia took a feed sack and wiped the dust from Blaze's saddle. She fingered the rawhide thong that she used as a bridle for Cricket.

"I wish I had a bridle for Cricket," she muttered. "I'll be riding her until Eddie gets out of the Navy and she shouldn't have to wear this old rawhide."

"Well, we can't afford to buy one," Denny said grimly. "We'll be lucky if we make enough money to make the payment on the ranch this month. And no one is going to give you the money or donate you a bridle."

"Donate!" Claudia regarded Denny thoughtfully.

126

"But people do give things ... even little things." Her voice trailed off and she chewed on her thumb and her eyes narrowed as she looked off into space.

"Come on, Claudia, I have to get out to the track," Denny ordered. "If I do a good job today, I'm sure Mr. Pomeroy will let me exercise steady." They both glanced up as a car turned into the driveway.

Miss Butterfield's car squealed to a stop and she jumped out. "Thought I'd ride early today," she said brightly.

"We're going to the track to watch Denny ride some of Mr. Pomeroy's thoroughbreds," Claudia told her.

"Oh!" Miss Butterfield hesitated. "Do you suppose he would mind if I came along?" She blushed. "Would I be imposing?"

"Of course not," Denny assured her. "We'd be glad to have you."

"By the way, Alice Brown bought a lovely Arabian and she's going to have you board it," Miss Butterfield said.

"Gee, that's swell." Claudia clapped her hands. "See, everything is working out."

"We'll have to get ready for her," Denny said seriously. "Do you know when she wants to bring the horse here?"

"She'll call you," Miss Butterfield said. "Well, I'm ready to go."

It was quiet when Uncle Tom drove them down to the Pomeroy barn. Jonas Pomeroy was talking to a groom but when he saw them he walked over with quick steps. "Well, Denny, are you ready to gallop your first thoroughbred?"

"Yes, sir!" Denny said.

"It sure is quiet around here," Claudia said. "It isn't like Kendall's stables."

"Racing is a business," Jonas Pomeroy explained. "The grooms go about getting the horses ready for their morning gallops. Afterwards they are cooled out, brushed, watered, and put in their stalls to eat. Everyone has a job to do, and we like everything done quietly."

"Doesn't anyone have any fun?" Claudia wanted to know.

"Why, if you like what you're doing," Jonas Pomeroy smiled across at her, "I guess it can be called fun." He turned to smile at Miss Butterfield. "Well, have you come to look at your competition?"

"What do you mean?" Miss Butterfield stared at him with surprise.

"I mean you have a fine thoroughbred in Domino," Jonas Pomeroy said. "Has he ever been raced?"

"I really don't know," Miss Butterfield answered. "I bought him for a pleasure horse."

"Maybe we'll get a chance to find out." Jonas Pomeroy grinned at her. He turned to Denny. "If you get along all right on Blue Over maybe we can match him with Domino."

"That would be exciting," Claudia said.

"Blue Over is just a colt," Mr. Pomeroy went on. "He's only had a couple of months' training. But he's beginning to know what to do." He turned as a groom led a large, slim, bay thoroughbred up beside them. "He's learning how to hug a rail and he breaks well out of the gate."

"Do you think I could handle him?" Denny was excited.

128

"You'll get the feel of handling him after a few trials," Jonas Pomeroy assured him.

"I think I would like racing," Miss Butterfield said. "I've always wanted to do a race."

Claudia listened to them for a moment, gazed at the trim legs of the bay, and then her attention wandered toward the opened tops of the stall doors down the shed row. She began looking into the stalls and stopped to watch the sleek thoroughbreds munching hay. As she turned away her eye caught something bright on the ground. She stooped and picked up a dime. She looked quickly in Uncle Tom's direction but he was talking with Miss Butterfield and Jonas Pomeroy. She held it out on the flat of her hand. A groom came along, stared at her hand, grinned, and reached into his pocket. He dropped a second coin into her hand and stood with his hands on his hips.

"And now what are you going to do with so much money?"

"Oh, it isn't near enough," she explained. "I have to buy a bridle for my horse."

"Well, then." He dropped another dime into her hand and went whistling down the shed row. Claudia looked after him thoughtfully. Then she began watching the ground as she walked along. Two men stood talking and Claudia hesitated as she scanned the ground around them.

"What are you looking for?" one of them asked.

"A dime," she announced brightly, searching carefully.

"Here, this ought to make up for your lost dime." One of the men reached into his pocket and brought out a quarter. Claudia hesitated. "Come on, take it." He turned to the other man. "Come on, Jake, give the girl something." Jake grinned and put fifty cents in her hand.

"Oh, thank you." Claudia counted the money slowly and put it in her pocket.

"Now, are you happy?" Jake asked.

"I haven't nearly enough yet," Claudia said seriously. "I'm going to buy a bridle for my horse." Both men laughed.

"That beats anything I ever heard," Jake roared. "Here, that idea deserves a dollar." He pulled out his wallet and plunked a dollar bill in Claudia's hand. She thanked him hurriedly and skipped down the shed row.

There were eight long barns and Claudia walked completely around each one. As she searched in front of each stall she looked long and carefully as she met the grooms and trainers. They all asked if she'd lost money and each time she explained about the bridle. The grooms laughed and dropped dimes in her hands. Almost every trainer gave her fifty cents until her small jean pocket began to show a bulge.

When she came around the last barn she saw Miss Butterfield and Uncle Tom walking toward the track. She stopped, once more, and counted the money. Six dollars! She shoved it quickly into her pocket. She joined them and they hurried along the lane that led to the track. Claudia's pocket jingled as she walked.

"What do you have in your pocket, Claudia?" Uncle Tom observed the bulge.

"Money." Claudia was matter of fact.

"Where did you get it?" Uncle Tom stopped and stared at her.

"It was donated," Claudia announced. "There're the nicest people around horses." She giggled nervously. "Some didn't even ask, they just gave it to me and when the others knew I was trying to get a bridle for Cricket they even gave me fifty-cent pieces."

"What are you talking about?" Uncle Tom's face showed his concern. Claudia explained about the first dime and how she got the rest of the money. Uncle Tom regarded her for a moment and then threw his head back and roared with laughter.

"Well, really, Uncle Tom." Miss Butterfield didn't smile. "I'm sure Claudia's mother wouldn't approve."

"I'm sure she wouldn't," Uncle Tom agreed. "But this beats everything!"

"Will I have to give it back?" Claudia watched them anxiously.

"Do you think you could?" Uncle Tom chuckled.

"I'd never remember everybody." Claudia shook her head grimly. "I'd just never remember."

"Well, then," Uncle Tom admitted, "we have a problem."

"I won't do it again," Claudia promised. "Anyway, I have enough to get Cricket a bridle. You know, Uncle Tom, if everyone would just donate a dime you could help an awful lot of people."

"That's right, Claudia," Uncle Tom told her. "But when one person gets the benefit that is selfish. When everyone is helped it is charity."

"Indeed so," Miss Butterfield agreed. "I hope you understand that, Claudia."

"Oh, I do." Claudia glanced quickly at Uncle Tom and her face retained its soberness when he didn't smile.

"Couldn't we stop by the saddlery and buy the bridle before we go home?" Claudia begged.

Uncle Tom looked at her for a long moment. "We'll have to hurry if we expect to watch Denny ride his first thoroughbred." He quickened his step and Claudia hesitated and then fell into step beside him.

When they reached the track Jonas Pomeroy was standing beside the bay thoroughbred. Denny sat balanced on the small exercise saddle listening to Mr. Pomeroy's instructions. They watched him face the horse down the track and start him in an easy canter for a short distance and then let him out in a hand gallop.

Claudia pulled at Uncle Tom's sleeve. "About the bridle..."

"Shhhhh." Uncle Tom shook his head and Claudia frowned. She watched Denny for a few minutes and then turned to Uncle Tom again. "Did he warm him up already?" Claudia watched him soberly but her face relaxed when he smiled down at her.

"Yes." Uncle Tom gave his attention to watching Denny. As Denny rounded the first turn he let Blue Over out a little. They watched Denny keep a firm grip on the reins as he sped down the straightaway. As he reached the three-quarter pole he tried pulling Blue Over up, but the bay came on.

"Is he running away?" Claudia asked nervously.

"No," Jonas Pomeroy told her. "Blue Over likes to go all the way around the track. Denny is holding him in very well." They watched Denny bring Blue Over around the

132

far turn. He galloped past them and then brought Blue Over back, quieting the anxious horse. Blue Over's nostrils were dilated, his eyes bright, and he danced with quick steps. Denny was smiling as Blue Over tossed his head.

"Did I handle him all right?" Denny wanted to know. "He sure wants to run."

"You did fine," Jonas Pomeroy assured him. "All you need is experience."

"It's a real thrill to ride a fast horse," Denny said excitedly. "I can't explain it."

"He wasn't going as fast as he can, Denny," Uncle Tom told him.

"I know," Denny agreed. "I guess that would be even more of a thrill."

"That's something I've always wanted to do," Miss Butterfield said.

"All right," Jonas Pomeroy addressed himself to her, "how about a match race between Blue Over and Domino?"

"Are you really serious?" Miss Butterfield stared at him. "When you first mentioned it I thought you were joking." She was thoughtful. "It really wouldn't be fair. I've never raced Domino."

"I'd let Denny ride Blue Over," Jonas Pomeroy told her. "He's never run competition yet either. It might be interesting to see what they can do."

"It would be exciting," Miss Butterfield agreed. "When shall we do it?"

"How about tomorrow morning?" Jonas Pomeroy said.

"That would be all right with me. Tomorrow is a holiday," Denny said. "Just as long as I get to Mr. Kendall's by noon."

"Do you think you can get up early again, Claudia?" Uncle Tom chuckled.

"If Denny is going to race I can," Claudia retorted.

"I'll pull the trailer for you," Uncle Tom offered, "with my pickup truck."

"Oh, good," Miss Butterfield said. "I don't have a trailer hitch on my car." She smiled at Jonas Pomeroy. "I've been working Domino every day but I think I'll work him a little harder today."

"We're planning on winning, eh, Denny?" Jonas Pomeroy slapped Denny on the leg and smiled up at him.

"Yes, sir!" Denny said briskly. He turned Blue Over toward the stables and Claudia took Uncle Tom's arm as they walked along. Miss Butterfield stood talking to Jonas Pomeroy.

"Don't tell Mom about the money," Claudia whispered.

"I won't," Uncle Tom promised. "I'm going to let you tell her." Claudia looked startled, frowned, and then ran to the pickup truck. She climbed in and sat down. Uncle Tom stood for a moment, chuckled, and went to join Jonas and Miss Butterfield. Claudia leaned out the window and watched Uncle Tom. A frown creased her forehead and she bit her lip thoughtfully. Uncle Tom would see to it that she told her mother about the money. Long ago Denny and Claudia discovered that Uncle Tom was strong on honesty. She sighed and tried to think about the race to-morrow.

It wasn't necessary to waken Denny the next morning. He fed the horses before he called Claudia. They hurriedly ate breakfast and were cleaning the stables when Uncle Tom drove into the yard with Sam Kendall's trailer behind his pickup truck.

"We're almost ready to go," Denny told him. "Where's Miss Butterfield?"

"It's still early," Uncle Tom said. "Is there any coffee made?"

"Mom is still asleep, Uncle Tom," Denny said. "I don't know how to make it."

"I'll make some while we're waiting for Miss Butterfield." Uncle Tom started for the house. Just then Miss Butterfield's car turned into the driveway. Uncle Tom went to meet her. "I was just getting ready to make a pot of coffee."

"I could use a cup," Miss Butterfield said. "I just couldn't eat a thing this morning. I kept thinking about Domino." She regarded Denny a moment. "Aren't you excited?"

"It's more than that," Denny replied. "If I should win it might prove to Mr. Pomeroy that I can handle his horses."

"I really don't expect Domino to win," Miss Butterfield said. "After all, I don't have any experience racing. And I don't know how fast Domino can run."

"Well, it's just a match race," Uncle Tom said. "It's all in fun."

"We'll be finished with the chores in a few minutes," Denny said.

"All right," Uncle Tom replied. "When you've done the stables, load Domino and we'll be ready to go."

Denny was fastening the tail gate when Uncle Tom and

Miss Butterfield came out of the house. "We're ready, Uncle Tom."

When they arrived at the Pomeroy barns a groom was wiping Blue Over's sleek coat with a flannel cloth. Denny jumped from the pickup truck and ran over to speak to Jonas Pomeroy. Uncle Tom backed Domino out of the trailer and fastened his lead rope to a ring on the truck. He put the saddle on Domino and buckled the straps firmly.

Claudia ran her hand over the flat seat of the English saddle. "I've raced bareback on Blaze," she said, "but never with a flat saddle."

"Anyone who can ride bareback won't have trouble with a flat saddle," Miss Butterfield said. "When I was your age, Claudia, I had to learn to ride bareback before I was allowed to have a saddle."

"I liked riding Domino the other day," Claudia said. "He's easy to handle."

"Well," Miss Butterfield smiled at her and tucked her wispy hair into the knot at the back of her head, "maybe someday you can race him, too."

"Are you ready?" Denny called.

"Right," Uncle Tom answered. He led Domino around and then tested the cinch again. "He's ready, Miss Butterfield."

"I think you'd better warm them a little," Jonas Pomeroy suggested. "Walk them around the courtyard until they're loosened up and then we'll go out on the track." He turned to Uncle Tom. "We'll start down near the three-quarter pole and race past the grandstand. That's a good sprint."

"Claudia," Miss Butterfield called, "would you like to warm Domino?"

"Oh, could I?" Claudia turned to Uncle Tom and he led Domino over and gave her a boost into the saddle. He shortened the stirrups and Claudia walked him out.

Miss Butterfield, Uncle Tom, and Jonas Pomeroy stood under the shed row while Denny and Claudia walked the horses around the barn area. After a while they trotted them and then urged them into a slow canter. "This is fun," Claudia called to them.

"They should be all right now," Jonas Pomeroy called. "Let's go out on the track and find out which is the faster horse."

"I'll have to get a scarf from my purse or my hair will blow in my face," Miss Butterfield said. "I'd hate to lose the race by a hair." She chuckled. Claudia giggled and sat holding Domino quiet.

Miss Butterfield hurried toward the pickup truck. Opening the door, she climbed into the seat and reached for her purse. She tied the scarf around her hair and then jumped down from the running board. Suddenly she crumpled to the ground and grasped her ankle with both hands. She rocked back and forth and moaned with pain.

Uncle Tom ran to her side and helped her to her feet. She tried to take a step and winced in pain. "I'm afraid it's sprained," she cried.

"That's too bad," Jonas Pomeroy said. "I have some tape in the tack room. I'll fix it up for you in a jiffy." He hurried down the shed row, disappeared behind a door, and soon came back with a three-inch roll of adhesive tape. He sat Miss Butterfield down on the running board and

Uncle Tom carefully removed her boot. Claudia and Denny sat on their horses, watching quietly. "Just starting to swell. We'll get this support on and then you get your foot up and I think we can prevent any further swell-

ing." He strapped her ankle skillfully. "I'm afraid you won't be wearing a shoe for a day or two."

"Oh, I don't mind that." Miss Butterfield watched Jonas smooth the adhesive well up on the calf of her leg. "That feels better already." She sighed and leaned back. Then she sat bolt upright. "I almost forgot. The race! I can't ride!"

138

12. THE WINNER

THEY all stood in silence when Miss Butterfield made the exclamation. Her appealing glance traveled from face to face.

"You mean we can't race?" Denny cried as he pulled Blue Over up beside her.

"We can race another day," Jonas Pomeroy said calmly.

"It's only a match race," Uncle Tom assured them. "It isn't that important."

"But we wanted to find out who is the fastest horse," Claudia protested. She stroked Domino's neck. They sat silently, contemplating the situation.

"Why don't you ride him, Claudia?" Miss Butterfield clasped her hands together hopefully.

"Oh, could I?" Claudia sat up straight and looked at Uncle Tom.

"That wouldn't be fair," Denny said. "Claudia hasn't run Domino yet."

"I cantered him," Claudia said. "What's the difference if I go a little faster?"

"Well, I haven't raced him either," Miss Butterfield said. "I'm sure Claudia could handle him as well as I."

"I don't know . . ." Uncle Tom hesitated. He scratched his chin thoughtfully.

139

"She can do it, I know she can," Miss Butterfield begged.

"It's entirely up to you folks," Jonas Pomeroy said. "I'll race Blue Over. This is just an interesting match race to me."

"I don't think Claudia rides well enough," Denny interrupted.

"I do so," Claudia bit off the words. "You're afraid I'll beat you."

"I'm not either," Denny said quickly. "I just don't want you to feel bad."

"I won't feel bad," Claudia began on a teasing note. "I just want to ride Domino and prove I'm a better rider."

"All right," Denny agreed. "Don't say I didn't warn you." He turned to Uncle Tom. "How about it, Uncle Tom?"

"I wonder if your mother would approve," Uncle Tom muttered.

"Of course she wouldn't." Claudia grinned. "But Mom doesn't understand horses the way we do." She smiled at Denny. "She'd worry about anything we did. Anyway, we just have to race."

"Well," Uncle Tom said slowly, "I guess it will be all right."

"O.K., Denny," Jonas Pomeroy said. "Come along and I'll give you your instructions."

"Do I get some instructions, too?" Claudia faced Miss Butterfield.

"Well," Miss Butterfield began, "I don't know what to say." She studied the ground, leaned forward, and rubbed her ankle gently. "Just hold him firmly and talk to him

140

when you need to go faster. Keep him straight and don't let him veer out on that first turn.''

''The race will be over before we reach the first turn,'' Claudia told her.

''I guess that's right,'' Miss Butterfield agreed. ''Well, all I can say is do your best.''

The two horses walked out on the track and lined up at the far end. Jonas Pomeroy and Uncle Tom made a seat with their hands and Miss Butterfield sat on them and put her arms around their necks. They carried her to the track and made her comfortable in the bleachers. She propped her ankle up and settled back to watch. Then Jonas Pomeroy and Uncle Tom hurried down to the track.

Jonas Pomeroy drew a line across the track with the toe of his boot and advised the youngsters about trying to start from a standstill. Uncle Tom walked up the track, past the grandstand, to the far end and near the first turn. There he drew a line across the tanbark and then waved his arm that he was ready.

''When I drop my arm down, start,'' Jonas Pomeroy told them. Denny edged Blue Over toward the line, pulling him around as he danced backwards. Claudia walked Domino up slowly and stopped. ''One . . . two . . . three . . . GO!'' Jonas Pomeroy's arm swung down swiftly and the two horses leaped forward, gathered speed, and ran neck and neck. Their strides matched so closely that they appeared as one. Claudia leaned over Domino's neck and shifted her weight. Domino veered to one side and his shoulder bumped Denny's leg. Claudia shot Denny an uneasy look.

141

"Stay over, Claudia. What are you trying to do? Get over!" Denny yelled.

"I'm sorry," Claudia yelled back and pulled Domino wide.

Denny pushed Blue Over forward with a burst of speed and he left Domino a length behind. He grinned back at Claudia and leaned low over Blue Over's withers. Claudia flailed her heels into Domino's sides and shouted over his neck, "Come on, Domino, come on, let's go!"

Domino lengthened his stride and started to close the gap between the two horses. Denny turned with a startled glance and tried to get more speed from Blue Over as Domino moved up. They neared the grandstand. Claudia pressed hard against the iron stirrups and tightened her knees as she leaned forward to give Domino his head.

"Hah! Hah!" Denny yelled at Blue Over. The tanbark flew out from under the pounding hoofs in little spurts as the horses stretched for more speed. Suddenly Domino pulled ahead, and they crossed the line with Blue Over's nose even with Domino's neck. It was over. Uncle Tom walked to the middle of the track and stood looking after them. Jonas Pomeroy hurried up the track with short bobbing steps as he watched the youngsters start to pull the horses up when they rounded the first turn.

Claudia allowed Domino to slow by himself but Denny fought to pull Blue Over to a stop. Denny stood in his stirrups but he was almost at the back stretch before he got Blue Over under control. He cantered him slowly around the track toward the gates leading to the barns. Claudia brought Domino back and stopped him in front of the grandstand. She waited as Miss Butterfield hobbled down the steps of the grandstand, bracing herself with a broomstick. Uncle Tom went to help her. Claudia looked down the track.

Denny was walking Blue Over in small circles and staring up the track at the small group around Domino.

"You rode him beautifully, dear," Miss Butterfield said, stroking Domino's neck. "I couldn't have done better."

"He's not hard to stop," Claudia told her. "And I was glad for that." She glanced up the track again at Denny. "I think I would have been scared on Blue Over."

143

"He's just a colt," Jonas Pomeroy said. "He still needs lots of work. I can see what he needs now. This was good for him."

"I'll bet Denny is mad," Claudia said, uneasily.

"He shouldn't be," Jonas Pomeroy told her. "Blue Over needs to be worked with another horse. Denny handled him all right." Jonas Pomeroy patted Claudia's hand. "That was a good match. You rode Domino with good hands."

"Oh, thank you, Mr. Pomeroy." Claudia smiled down at him. "Let's go down and see Denny." She clucked to Domino. "He tried very hard to beat me; and I thought he would win, too."

"He rode a good race," Uncle Tom said. Claudia trotted on ahead. Denny didn't look up as she approached.

He rode with his head down on his chest and he didn't speak when Claudia put Domino in step beside him.

"Wasn't that exciting, Denny?" Claudia smiled at him.

"It was all right," he muttered.

"You're not mad because I won, are you?" Claudia wrinkled her forehead with worry.

"Of course not!" Denny snapped.

"I'm glad I won," Claudia went on, "but I wouldn't have minded if you had."

"I'm glad too." Denny looked straight at her. "Only ..."

"Only what, Denny?" Claudia wanted to know.

"I make a mess of everything I do." Denny faced her. "I flubbed the trail ride for Mr. Kendall. Now I've lost a race for Mr. Pomeroy."

"But this was just a match race," Claudia insisted. "It

was all in fun.'' She peered at him closely. ''If it had been important they wouldn't have let me ride.'' Denny studied her face for a moment and the frown left his brow. ''Mr. Pomeroy was pleased with the way you handled Blue Over. He said it showed that Blue Over has the makings of a good racer.'' Denny shrugged his shoulders and gave her a smile.

''I guess you're right.'' He pulled Blue Over to a stop. ''I did want to prove I could do it.'' He turned as Jonas Pomeroy and Uncle Tom walked up. ''Is Mr. Pomeroy angry?'' he whispered to Claudia.

''I told you he wasn't. Honest,'' she said quickly.

''Well, what did you think of your first race?'' Jonas Pomeroy grinned up at Denny.

''Not so good,'' Denny admitted.

''You did very well,'' Mr. Pomeroy told him. ''You kept him going straight, which is important.'' He laid a hand on Blue Over's neck. ''Remember that Domino is an older, wiser horse.'' This brought a smile from Miss Butterfield. ''Blue Over is going to be a runner, but he needs experience. I'll let you exercise him and you'll learn how to pilot him down a track.''

''You'll have to learn how to come out of a starting gate,'' Uncle Tom put in.

Denny looked at Uncle Tom and then back at Jonas Pomeroy. ''You mean you still want me to work for you?''

''Of course, I want you to work for me,'' Jonas Pomeroy said. ''You handle a horse well and that's what I want in an exercise boy.''

''That's swell, Denny,'' Claudia said quickly. ''Maybe

we can have a match race again." She smiled at him. "The next time you'll know so much you'll win."

"This was worth a sprained ankle," Miss Butterfield said.

"I wish you could have ridden Domino, though," Claudia said.

"I'm glad you were around," Miss Butterfield told her.

"Maybe we should have a doctor look at that ankle," Uncle Tom suggested.

"Oh, no." Miss Butterfield looked down at the bandaged ankle. "There's hardly any swelling. Mr. Pomeroy did a good job of strapping it." She smiled across at him. "I think if I just get off my feet it will be all right."

"We'd better get home," Uncle Tom suggested. "Denny has to go to work for Mr. Kendall. Let's get Domino loaded."

"I have to walk him out," Claudia announced. "He's still warm."

"Me too," Denny said, as he led Blue Over around the oval in front of the barns. The youngsters talked as they walked the horses.

"That's what I like to see." Jonas Pomeroy rubbed his chin in thought. "Those children have a feeling for horses. Every good horseman has it."

The children walked their horses until they were cool and then Denny helped unsaddle Blue Over. Uncle Tom loaded Domino into the trailer, and they all waved good-by to Jonas Pomeroy as they turned onto the highway.

When Claudia and Denny reached home they jumped out of the car and started toward the house. "Come on, Miss Butterfield, we're going to tell Mom." She waved them on and hobbled over and sat down under the pepper tree. Claudia burst into the kitchen. "Mom, I won the race!" Their mother put her coffee cup down and looked at them aghast.

"What race?" she addressed herself to Denny. "What is Claudia talking about?"

"We just had a match race," Denny went on to explain.

"You didn't race, did you, Claudia?" Her mother regarded her with disbelief. "You didn't race?"

"I won, Mom," Claudia insisted.

"I just don't like this." Their mother shook her head. "Where's Uncle Tom?"

"He's putting Domino away," Claudia told her. "You see, Mom, Miss Butterfield sprained her ankle. I just had to ride."

"Uncle Tom wasn't going to let Claudia race but we talked him into it," Denny said as Uncle Tom walked in the door.

"How could you let a little girl like Claudia race a horse?" She gave him a severe glance.

"These children are doing things they'll never forget," Uncle Tom reminded her.

"I know, but suppose they get hurt," their mother said sharply.

"But we haven't," Claudia reminded her.

"Mom, we want to have all the fun we can," Denny said seriously. "The next time Mr. Davis brings people to look at the ranch they may buy it."

"You're right, we do have to face that," his mother said.

"Oh, don't even talk about it," Claudia said grimly.

147

"We have to talk about it," her mother said. "So far we've just been able to make the payments each month, but there is nothing sure." She frowned at Uncle Tom. "I certainly don't want any accidents on top of all our other troubles."

"Oh, Mom," Denny protested.

"Now you know I wouldn't let those children do something I thought they couldn't do," Uncle Tom said.

"I guess I do know that, I'm sorry." She smiled at him. "Sometimes I think you are as much of a child as they are."

"Now, Mom, you know Uncle Tom knows all about horses," Denny went on.

"That may be so," his mother agreed, "but he may not know all about children."

"I guess I'd better go to the stables." Denny jumped to his feet. "Mr. Kendall won't like it if I'm late."

"Are you going to ride Blaze?" Claudia wanted to know.

"Yes, I'll get him saddled." Denny turned to go. His mother walked to the door with him. "Why, there's Miss Butterfield sitting in the lawn chair. Why didn't you ask her in?"

"We did," Claudia said. "She wanted to sit with her ankle up for a while."

"I'll take her a cup of coffee." Their mother went back into the kitchen and soon returned with the coffee. "How's your ankle?" she asked, handing the cup to Miss Butterfield.

"It feels better," Miss Butterfield said. "The swelling

148

is going down." She cocked her head and listened. "Isn't that your telephone ringing?" They listened. Uncle Tom walked up and hearing the phone he hurried toward the back door.

He poked his head out the back door. "Miss Brown wants to bring a horse out to board. Shall I say yes?"

"Yes!" Claudia yelled and grinned at her mother who nodded her head and looked with embarrassment at Miss Butterfield. Denny came running over when he heard Claudia.

"Is it another boarder? Who is it?" He was excited.

"Don't you remember Alice Brown said she was going to call?" Miss Butterfield said.

"Now, everything's all right," Claudia stated. "Can't we call Mr. Davis and tell him not to bother about selling the ranch?"

"Not until we see if things are really going to be better," her mother told her. "I'd have to hear from your father before I took the ranch off the market."

"We ought to write and tell him," Claudia insisted.

"I'm sure things will work out," Miss Butterfield said. "This is such a nice ranch."

"Gee, now we'll have to put Cricket and Blaze in the same stall for a while." Claudia stood thinking, her forefinger pressed at the corner of her mouth. "It will work, though."

"Denny, you'd better go, you'll be late and Mr. Kendall won't like it if you're late," his mother said. Denny glanced uneasily toward the house when Uncle Tom slammed the back door, and came out smiling.

"That was Miss Brown, she's bringing a horse here for you to board," Uncle Tom said.

"Now we'll have to think of stalls," Denny muttered.

"Right now we'll think about the new boarder we're getting," Claudia said.

13. BARBED WIRE

THE sun was high in the sky. There were few shadows by the framework of the new stall. Uncle Tom went about picking up the small pieces of scrap lumber that littered the ground. It would take just a little more work to make a good third stall.

"Well, let's get Cricket moved in with Blaze then," Denny said. "I hope they get along so they won't give us any trouble."

"Cricket wouldn't fight with anybody," Claudia put in.

"Gee, we're lucky to get another boarder." Denny was thoughtful. "If we can manage the payment this time, then next month we can finish the new stall and make Blaze's into a double. Cricket can stay with him."

"Yes, that will work," Uncle Tom assured him. "Miss

Brown will be here any minute. Sam Kendall is bringing the horse over for her.''

''Does Miss Brown's horse kick, too?'' Claudia wanted to know.

''I hardly think so,'' Miss Butterfield said.

''Well, then, I'd think she'd board it at Kendall's,'' Claudia said thoughtfully. ''He would take all the best ones.''

''He hasn't any more stalls for rent,'' Denny said. ''He's lucky enough to be full up.''

''Well, I wish we were,'' Claudia mused. ''Wouldn't that be something?'' They all sat around Miss Butterfield and began to talk about the race.

''I would like the thrill of running one race with Domino,'' Miss Butterfield said. ''But I don't think I ever will.''

''Why?'' Claudia turned a disappointed face toward her. ''I was hoping I could race again.''

''First of all,'' Miss Butterfield explained, ''I bought Domino for a pleasure horse. If I continued to race him he might become speed crazy, then he would no longer be a pleasure.''

''She's right,'' Uncle Tom agreed. ''When you have a good horse you have to decide what you want to do most with him. Race horses aren't much good for anything else and a show horse is no good for racing.'' He grinned at her. ''Of course there are exceptions.''

''Blaze would never be spoiled,'' Denny bragged. ''But I'm only going to do a hundred-yard dash with him once in a while.'' He stared down the road. ''Here comes Mr.

151

Kendall.'' They watched the trailer bump along the driveway.

The gray horse braced herself when the trailer came to an abrupt stop. Alice Brown jumped down from the running board of the pickup truck and ran over to Miss Butterfield. ''Oh, Agatha, I found the most beautiful Arabian mare, not a blemish on her,'' she exclaimed excitedly. ''Come, see her.''

''Lead her over here. I don't want to get up for a while yet.'' Miss Butterfield pointed to her bound ankle.

''Did you get hurt on Domino?'' Alice Brown's eyes widened and she put her hands on her hips. ''I knew that horse was too much for you. Now, if you had listened to me.''

Miss Butterfield looked at Alice Brown's red hair and gave her an exasperated glance. ''You always jump to conclusions!'' Miss Brown frowned down at her, pushed her hair back from her freckled face, and turned away. Uncle Tom put the tail gate down and Sam backed the dappled gray mare out of the trailer. The mare was almost white, with round splotches of gray dapples covering her back and flanks. Her round brown eyes were soft and intelligent. Miss Brown took the lead rope from Sam and led the gray over to Miss Butterfield. ''She's lovely.'' She ran a finger up and down the velvety nose.

They stood around admiring the mare, while Alice Brown ran up and down the yard showing the fine action as the gray trotted and pranced beside her, tossing her head so that the white mane waved like a silver scarf. She finally brought the horse to a stop, led her to the edge of the lawn, and loosened the lead rope. The mare stretched her neck and began to nibble at the grass.

"I'll put her away now," Miss Brown said, then added, "I found a good, used, flat saddle. I'm going to buy it."

"Then we can go on rides together," Miss Butterfield said. "It will be nice boarding our horses at the same place, so handy."

"I have just enough time to run down and get the saddle before lunch." Miss Brown looked at her watch and then at Denny. "Would you put her up for me?"

"Why don't we put Cricket and your horse out in the pasture?" Claudia suggested. "They can get acquainted until Denny comes home with Blaze."

"Yeah, we'd better be getting down to the stable," Sam Kendall said. "Suppose I load Blaze into the trailer and we'll take off."

"O.K. by me," Denny said. He led Blaze out of the stable and handed the lead rope to Mr. Kendall. Blaze walked willingly into the trailer and stood quietly while Sam Kendall tied him. Denny went to get his saddle and tossed it into the back of the pickup truck.

"What's the mare's name?" Denny smiled across at Alice Brown.

"Silver Wings," she answered. "Isn't that beautiful?"

"Oh, I like that," Claudia cried. "Turn her into the pasture while I get Cricket." She hesitated. "Cricket has a beautiful name too. Revel's Duchess, but we call her Cricket." Claudia flicked her pony tail with a turn of her head and her shoulders set proudly. She hurried to the stable and brought Cricket to the pasture gate. Uncle Tom opened the gate and the youngsters turned the horses loose.

They stood for a moment and Cricket walked cautiously over to Silver Wings and extended her muzzle. She sniffed and snorted loudly but her ears pointed forward with a friendly gesture. Silver Wings wiggled her nose and blew noisily, then whirled and, with tail up and mane flying, went galloping across the pasture. Cricket boggled her head, tossed her heels, and ran after her. They raced across the pasture and dashed around to come back to stand blowing at the gate. Then they were off again.

"Aren't they having fun?" Claudia stood on the lower rail of the fence and hung her elbows over the top.

"She'll have a nice spot here," Sam Kendall said. "I'd like to have more time to let my boarders out for a good run in my pastures but I have every stall rented and it keeps us busy cleaning. Shall we go, Denny?"

"I guess we'd better," Denny said. "I'm glad I'm with my boss." He grinned at Mr. Kendall. "If I'm late he'll be with me." Denny started to climb into the pickup truck. He stood on the running board and looked out at the pasture. The horses were at the far corner, down by the walnut tree. Denny turned the door handle and then stopped. "Hey! Something's wrong with the horses!"

Denny and Sam ran to the fence. Cricket was pulling back on something that appeared to be imprisoning her left front leg. She leaped about on her hind legs and bit at her left front ankle.

"It's that barbed wire in the corner," Claudia shouted. "I forgot about it!" Claudia climbed over the fence and ran across the field. Denny jumped down from the pickup truck and ran to the stable for the wirecutters. He handed them to Uncle Tom and ran quickly across the pasture while Sam and Uncle Tom followed. Claudia reached the little mare's side and tried to grab her halter. Cricket lunged.

"Get hold of her or she'll tear her leg to pieces," Sam Kendall told her. Claudia worked in close enough to grasp the halter, and when the little mare heard Claudia's soothing voice she stopped and stood shaking.

"Oh, I hope she isn't hurt," Claudia cried. "I was going to ask Uncle Tom to take this wire away, but I forgot."

Uncle Tom reached down and tried to lift the little mare's foot out of the ring of wire. Cricket jumped. Claudia put her hand on Cricket's nose and drew the mare's head tight against her chest. Tears filled her eyes when she saw the blood on Uncle Tom's hands.

"Gosh, Uncle Tom, is it bad?" Denny held the wire while Uncle Tom applied the wirecutters. Sam Kendall eased the cut ends away and then pulled the wire from under Cricket until she stood free.

"She has some nasty cuts," Sam Kendall said. "We'd better get her to the house and get an antiseptic on quick."

"She's bleeding!" Claudia cried. "It's all my fault. What will Eddie Binder say! He won't let me keep Cricket."

"It isn't that bad," Uncle Tom said. "We just have to hope there won't be any infection." He examined the area just above the hoof. "She has a number of lacerations but I don't think they will make her lame." Uncle Tom stood up and Silver Wings walked over to smell of him. He reached up to push her away and Denny gasped. Uncle

Tom glanced at him quickly and then followed his frightened gaze to Silver Wings' chest. Across the smooth white chest was a long, angry scratch. Sam Kendall and Claudia saw the scratch almost as soon as Denny did.

"Oh! Look at Silver Wings." Claudia pointed.

"Oh, my gosh!" Denny sputtered. "What will Miss Brown say?"

"This isn't serious." Sam Kendall examined the scratch. "Nothing to worry about here. It's torn with the muscle, I don't think it will even leave a scar."

"Is it as bad as Cricket's?" Claudia wanted to know.

"Oh, no," he assured her. "It looks worse than it is. If Silver Wings wasn't so white you wouldn't notice it much."

"Well, Miss Brown will notice it." Denny groaned and wiped his forehead. "This would have to happen on the very first day."

"Oh!" Claudia put her hands to the sides of her head. "I'm the one who suggested putting the horses out in the pasture!"

"It isn't anyone's fault," Uncle Tom told her.

"I wish I'd remembered about this darned ol' wire," Claudia said. "It's all my fault, all my fault!"

"No, it isn't," Uncle Tom tried to reassure her. "There's always wire and old lumber and nails to clean up when you move on a place. We'll just have to look around the pasture and see that there isn't any more."

"Let's get these horses up to the stable. Maybe if Cricket's leg is taken care of right away she won't have an infection." Uncle Tom motioned Claudia to lead the little mare, and Claudia walked her slowly across the pas-

156

ture. Uncle Tom brought Silver Wings. Denny and Sam Kendall trudged along behind him.

"We're always having bad luck," Denny muttered.

"Don't let it worry you, Denny." Sam Kendall clapped him on the shoulder. "This is just one of the risks of running a stable. Horses are always getting banged, scratched, or something. All you can do is try to keep everything in repair, keep everything clean, and hope for the best."

"I know Miss Brown is going to be angry." Denny was worried.

"Probably," Sam Kendall admitted. "You just have to face these things."

When Alice Brown saw Uncle Tom leading Silver Wings she hurried toward the fence. As they drew closer and she could see the angry red scratch her hand flew to her mouth and her forehead creased in a frown.

"Is she hurt? Oh, that beautiful horse, she's ruined!" She ran to examine the scratch.

"It's really not serious," Uncle Tom assured her. "In a few days you won't be able to see it."

"I can see for myself, and it's deep." She glared at the ring of faces around her. "Silver Wings didn't have a blemish on her. Five minutes on this place and look at her! Well, I won't leave her here to be torn up." She whirled on Sam Kendall. "I want a stall at your place. You surely can make room."

"I don't have a stall for rent," Sam told her. "Now, Miss Brown, this isn't serious. It's something that could happen anywhere, even if you had your own stable."

"I'm awfully sorry," Denny spoke up. "We're trying to have everything just right but we've been working on

158

stalls and I guess we didn't think about barbed wire in the pasture.''

"Well," Miss Brown exploded, "I don't want to worry every minute about my horse getting killed or injured.'' She pushed a lock of red hair back from her forehead. "You're responsible for the care of my horse!''

"Alice Brown!" Miss Butterfield hobbled over to the fence. "Why don't you be quiet and come to your senses?" she scolded. "They're not responsible for what your horse does and you know it. You always make a big production out of everything.''

"Well," Miss Brown snapped, "how would you like it if it were Domino?''

"I wouldn't like it if anything happened to Domino but I hope I would use my common sense," Miss Butterfield said evenly. "If I were these folks I'm not sure I would want to board your horse if you're going to make a fuss over something so trivial.''

"Trivial!" Alice Brown shouted. "Look at her smooth chest. It isn't smooth any longer.'' She shoved her hands deep in her pockets and turned on her heel. "I shall certainly find another stable.''

"I think you'd be better satisfied somewhere else,'' Uncle Tom said. He smoothed his mustache with quick motions and his eyes were narrow as he faced Alice Brown. She turned again to avoid his gaze.

"Oh, yes indeed,'' their mother put in. "We want everyone to be satisfied.''

Denny looked at his mother anxiously and then at Uncle Tom. "But we'd do our best,'' he insisted.

"Denny!" His mother shook her head at him. "Let Miss Brown decide."

"I have decided." She turned to Sam Kendall. "Will you please load my horse?"

Claudia led Cricket through the gate and Uncle Tom went to help her. Then he brought the antiseptic out of the stable and painted a streak across Silver Wings' scratch, careful to avoid Alice Brown's disapproving glance. He turned Cricket around and, bracing her foot against his knee, painted the punctures and lacerations just above the hoof.

"Is she going to be all right?" Claudia leaned over his shoulder and scanned the injured leg.

"It may swell and it will be pretty sore," he said. "If it doesn't become infected I don't think it will be serious. However, she may have a scar."

"I'll take good care of her, Uncle Tom," Claudia promised. "I'll keep her in the stall and when it heals I'll massage the place with olive oil so there won't be any scar."

"No, she must have exercise," Uncle Tom said. "You can't ride her but you'll have to see that she moves around. She can be put in pasture but you'll have to see that she keeps moving."

"If I lead her around every day ..." Claudia began.

"That's what I mean." Uncle Tom nodded. "Sometimes moving them around will keep the swelling down." He stood up and walked over to look at Silver Wings. She sniffed at his hand as he examined the scratch. Sam Kendall was fastening a lead rope to her halter.

"If I take her to my stable she'll have to be tied to a

160

hitch rack until you find a place for her," Sam told Miss Brown.

"That's all right," she answered grimly. "I'll find one."

"There's only one other stable that I know of," Uncle Tom put in. "I don't think much of it."

"I agree with you," Sam said.

"I can well afford to buy the kind of service I wish," Miss Brown said stiffly.

"But you can't afford to be obnoxious." Miss Butterfield thrust her chin out and adjusted her thick glasses. "I think you're going to be sorry."

Alice Brown studied Miss Butterfield's face a moment and she bit her lip thoughtfully as her gaze flicked from the faces of the two men and back to Miss Butterfield again. She tossed her head defiantly. "At least I shall find out." She turned to Sam Kendall. "May we go?"

Sam Kendall took Silver Wings to the back of the trailer and led her in. Denny sighed with resignation and gave a significant look to his mother. She smiled gently and put a comforting hand on his shoulder. Uncle Tom opened the car door and gave Alice Brown an arm into the seat. She flounced down on the cushion and sat stiffly, staring straight ahead. Denny seated himself gingerly beside her, hanging his elbow out the window. Without a word Sam climbed into the driver's seat and backed the trailer around.

Claudia stood holding Cricket by the halter, watching them go. "I guess we won't have to move Cricket, after all. We don't have a new boarder now."

14. SOLD

AFTER Alice Brown left the ranch Miss Butterfield hobbled over to Claudia and put an arm around her. "I'm sorry," she said. "I guess I didn't do a very good job getting you a boarder."

"It's just as well," Claudia's mother said. "I couldn't bear to have anyone unhappy here at the ranch." She cupped Claudia's chin in her fingers. "We have enough to worry about without having a dissatisfied boarder."

"I wish she'd stayed, though," Claudia murmured. She walked Cricket around and watched Uncle Tom pick up the barbed wire at the back of the pasture and roll it into a tight, barbed ball.

"I'll put this in my pickup truck and dispose of it," he said when he came back.

"Well, I've got to go," Miss Butterfield said, hobbling toward her car.

"Do you want me to drive you?" Uncle Tom offered.

"I can manage, thank you," Miss Butterfield said. "The swelling has gone down a bit. I think it will be all right in a few days if I keep it well bandaged." She drove slowly out of the yard. Claudia put Cricket in the pasture and then followed Uncle Tom and her mother into the house.

"I'm glad we have Miss Butterfield anyhow." Claudia was thoughtful. "Getting money is a real problem, isn't it?'' She looked up at her mother. ''And you have to have it every time you turn around.'' She scratched her chin. ''It's awful, you can't do anything without money.'' She frowned as she warmed up to her subject. ''I wish we could go back to the days when they used shells for money.''

''Well, if shells were money they would be just as hard to find,'' her mother said.

''Speaking of money...'' Uncle Tom gave Claudia a significant glance. She flushed, the red creeping slowly from the collar of her shirt. Claudia studied the ground, making little lines on the ground with the toe of her boot.

''What is it, Claudia?'' her mother wanted to know.

''Well.'' Claudia gave a long sigh. ''You see, I wanted a bridle and ... and.'' She glanced up at Uncle Tom. He stood waiting. ''And I didn't have the money for it ... and ... so ... I thought if everybody donated a dime ... it would be very simple ... and besides ... no one would ever miss a dime ... and I really didn't ask.'' She stopped.

''What is she talking about?'' her mother said anxiously.

''While we were at the race track Claudia walked around the barns getting ten cents or more from everyone who offered it to her,'' Uncle Tom explained.

''Why, Claudia Wolff!'' her mother said sharply. ''You know better than that. You go out to the stables and give all the money back.''

''I don't know who gave it to me,'' Claudia countered.

''You find every person and return the money.'' Her mother was firm.

"But, Mom, it was all donated," Claudia said quickly. "It was just like charity."

"Well, it isn't charity," her mother said. "So you'll give it back."

Claudia frowned and looked at Uncle Tom.

"You see, Claudia," Uncle Tom said. "It's better to work for what you get."

"I guess," Claudia agreed. "But I hardly have time to work for extra things now that we're so busy with the stables." She sighed again. "I baby sit just enough to help buy extra hay, let alone a bridle."

"You must remember that nothing comes easy that is worth-while," Uncle Tom said. "You'll just have to find something extra to do to buy things you want for yourself."

Claudia jumped to her feet when she heard the familiar roar of Jonas Pomeroy's sports car. Uncle Tom went to meet him and brought him into the kitchen.

"I have some good news for you, Claudia," he said jovially. "I have a letter from Eddie Binder and he is going to let you have Cricket for your own."

"Honest!" Claudia jumped to her feet. "How come?"

"He says here . . ." Jonas Pomeroy unfolded the letter. " 'I'm going to get married and have decided to make the Navy a career so I won't have a chance to raise ponies. I guess the deal I made with Claudia for her to have Cricket for the price of the first colt will stand. I'd like to give the pony to her outright, but we'll eventually need the money from the colt, I know. I am enclosing a bill of sale from me and Cricket's registration papers. Will you take care of them for Claudia?'" Jonas smiled down at her. "Now what do you think of that?"

"Cricket is really mine!" She whirled around to her mother. "Mom, Cricket is mine. I'm so glad!" Claudia danced about the kitchen and then stopped to look at the papers in her hand. "Revel's Duchess! Isn't that a beautiful name? But, of course, we'll still call her Cricket."

"Now remember, if you ever want to sell her I'll buy her," Jonas Pomeroy said, joking.

"Oh!" The smile faded from Claudia's face. "I don't think you'd want to buy her now."

"Why not?" Jonas Pomeroy wanted to know. He turned to Uncle Tom.

"She got caught in the barbed wire," Uncle Tom explained. "I don't think it will be serious."

"She's cut pretty bad," Claudia went on.

"Well, let's take a look at her." Jonas led the way out the back door. Claudia hesitated, gave a worried glance in her mother's direction, and then followed.

Uncle Tom opened the pasture gate, caught Cricket, and brought her back to Jonas Pomeroy. He picked up her front leg and examined it quietly. He stood up and pursed his lips thoughtfully.

"It might blemish her enough so she can't be shown in a horse show but it won't stop her from becoming a brood mare." He turned to Claudia. "I wouldn't worry about it. I think she'll heal all right."

"You mean you'd still buy her?" Claudia said.

"Of course." Jonas Pomeroy patted her shoulder. "You just let me know." He started toward his car.

165

"Well, I have to go. I just rushed over to tell you and leave the papers."

"Thank you, thank you for the papers," Claudia said quietly. She folded the papers and walked slowly toward the house. Uncle Tom followed Jonas Pomeroy to his car.

"Now you'll have something to show Denny when he comes home," her mother said, walking into the house behind her. Claudia didn't speak. She went to her room to put the papers away and then went back outside and hung on the pasture fence watching Cricket nibbling at the grass.

"No matter what happens," Claudia told her, "you'll always be my favorite horse. Of course I still like Blaze," she explained. "But it isn't the same." She looked toward the stable. Uncle Tom was working on the stall.

He nailed braces in the corners and tested the firmness of the framework, shaking it hard, but it was steady. Claudia went over to help him. They had nearly finished all the framing when Sam Kendall's pickup truck drove into the yard with the trailer attached.

"Gee, Mr. Kendall is bringing Denny and Blaze home," Claudia exclaimed, and then they saw Alice Brown step lightly down. Claudia gave Uncle Tom a questioning glance and walked over to meet them. Denny and Sam put the tail gate down. Denny led Blaze out of the trailer and trotted him toward the stable. Sam Kendall stood waiting by the trailer.

Their mother opened the door and came down the back steps. She looked surprised when she saw Alice Brown.

"Mrs. Wolff," Miss Brown began, "I owe you an apology." She took another breath. "I lost my temper. That

166

other stable was dirty and the horses were thin. I just couldn't leave Silver Wings in such a place." She paused. "I hope you'll forgive me and let me board Silver Wings here."

"Well, I guess it's all right," their mother said quietly. "I know the children will do their best but, of course, I don't want them upset." Sam Kendall backed Silver Wings out and handed the lead rope to Alice Brown. He fastened the tail gate and Uncle Tom went to help him. Miss Brown rubbed a hand along Silver Wings' neck.

"I gave Denny a month's board," she said quickly, then gave an embarrassed laugh as Uncle Tom and Sam Kendall walked over to join them. Denny came up grinning and took the lead rope from her.

"Let's go before you change your mind again." Sam chuckled.

"I won't change my mind," Alice said. "I'm rather ashamed of myself." She smiled at their mother. "I dread to face Agatha Butterfield." Sam took her by the arm and urged her toward the pickup truck. "I'll be out tomorrow afternoon." She smiled across at Uncle Tom. "I can ride her, can't I? I mean, the scratch isn't serious?"

"I told you the scratch wasn't serious," Uncle Tom said. "Of course you can ride her. It won't hurt her a bit."

"I'm forgiven then?" She looked around at all of them. She waved a hand at Claudia and stepped into the pickup truck. Denny came to stand beside his mother.

"We're lucky Miss Brown couldn't find a better place to keep her horse," Denny said briskly. "I don't think she'll find anything wrong again. At least, we'll be very careful."

"Well, things are looking up." Uncle Tom laughed. "Did you tell Denny what happened, Claudia?"

"About Cricket?" Her mother turned to Denny. "Claudia owns her now. She got the bill of sale today. Eddie Binder is getting married, so he gave Cricket to Claudia."

"Gee, that's wonderful," Denny said. "Now we're back where we were before."

"Now that she's mine," Claudia said anxiously, "may I keep her no matter what happens?"

"We've been through this before." Their mother sighed.

"You could go ahead and sell her now and we could keep the ranch for sure." Denny's voice held a hopeful note.

"Suppose you had to sell Blaze right now," Claudia snapped. "How would you like it?"

"Children, children!" their mother scolded. "We've been over this and you both know that if we have to give up the ranch we may not be able to keep either horse."

"But if we do move why couldn't we rent a place and take our boarders with us?" Denny suggested.

"Because we couldn't find another place equipped for horses." She put a hand on his shoulder. "You already know the struggle you've had to build what stabling you have. You couldn't do it all over again."

"I won't sell Cricket, I won't!" Claudia shouted.

"Claudia!" her mother ordered. "I allowed you to keep Cricket on the condition that she would have to go if we moved."

"What are we worrying about?" Denny spread his

hands. "We have two boarders, I'm working for Mr. Kendall. Why don't we telephone Dad and tell him we don't have to sell the ranch?"

"Because without your father's promotion we still couldn't manage," their mother explained. "You've both done well in trying to work things out but it isn't quite enough."

"But if Claudia sold Cricket ..." Denny began again.

"That would help for some time, I guess," their mother said uneasily. "But you can't make plans on uncertainties."

Uncle Tom joined them and stood listening as he lit his pipe.

"All I have to say," Claudia snapped, "is that everything is uncertain all the time. All I know," she continued, "is that I don't want to give up Cricket."

"Besides," their mother put in, "don't you remember what happened today?"

"What do you mean?" Denny said.

"You had a boarder this morning and then suddenly you didn't have a boarder." His mother went back on her heels and put her hands on her hips. "Things can happen just that fast."

"But we have the boarder again," Denny insisted.

"This is what makes life interesting," Uncle Tom chuckled. "Life is never dull when you have problems."

"Dull!" Claudia exploded. "Denny and I have so many problems. And I have the most. I'll never live to grow up!"

"Oh, I think you will." Uncle Tom chuckled. "But I'll

169

wager you'll know how to solve a problem by the time you're grown.''

"I think we've had quite a day." Their mother sighed wearily. "Let's get ready for supper, shall we?" She led the way to the house. "You're staying for supper, Uncle Tom?"

Claudia set the table while Denny and Uncle Tom discussed the building of the new stall. "I saw an old barn being torn down today," Uncle Tom said. "I think they're going to haul it away to the dump. Why don't I ask for the boards?"

"Yeah," Denny said. "That would close the stall in."

"I could paint it and then it would look as good as the rest of the stable," Claudia said. "We won't have to buy any paint either. I still have some left over from the last time we painted."

"It's probably all dried up," Denny commented.

"Maybe we can use some turpentine and thin it down," Uncle Tom said.

"Well, thank goodness for that," Denny retorted. "We can't spend any money right now." The telephone rang. Their mother picked up the receiver. She glanced quickly at Claudia and then at Denny. Claudia stood up and pressed her hands together.

"Certainly," their mother answered. "You may come right over, if you wish." She put the receiver down slowly. "Mr. Davis has another buyer for the ranch. He's bringing him over to look at it."

"Every time we make plans something happens," Denny muttered. "Might as well forget about those boards," he said aside to Uncle Tom.

"Maybe he won't like it," Claudia said hopefully. They were quiet as they ate supper. Claudia jumped to her feet when she heard the car drive into the yard. She ran to the back door.

"Claudia," her mother warned, "I don't want you to say anything." Claudia gave her a solemn look and didn't answer. They watched Mr. Davis show a tall, slim young man around the stable. Claudia ran from window to window following their progress.

"Oh, I hope he doesn't like it." Claudia's tone was wishful.

"Anyone would like this ranch," Denny said dully.

"They're coming in the house," Claudia whispered loudly.

When Mr. Davis stepped into the kitchen with the young man Claudia and Denny stood back quietly.

"You can see this is a well-planned ranch," Mr. Davis was saying.

"Well, I think I can put it to the use I want." He looked around. "I could convert the stables to chicken houses easily enough."

"Chicken houses!" Claudia gasped and ran to her room and slammed the door.

Denny glanced uneasily at his mother. "I guess I'd better go talk to her." And he left the room also.

When Denny opened the door Claudia was lying face down on her bed looking, dry-eyed, at the floor.

"We'll have Blaze," Denny began. "We bought him together, so we'll have him, no matter what."

"Things have always turned out right...." Claudia sat up. "But they really don't, do they, Denny?"

171

"I hear the car leaving." Denny looked out the window. "Maybe he didn't like the ranch, after all." Claudia jumped up and together they went to the kitchen. Uncle Tom sat smoking his pipe thoughtfully. He didn't look up. Their mother stood at the sink, looking out the window. She turned slowly as they came into the room.

"The young man is going to take the ranch," their mother said quietly. "He is putting a deposit down."

15. TRAIL'S END

THERE was shocked disbelief on the faces of Denny and Claudia when they realized that a deposit had been put down on the ranch. The ranch was sold. And it was going to be turned into a chicken ranch. The next morning breakfast was a solemn affair. Even Uncle Tom was not his usual jovial self but smoked angrily, puffing gray clouds from his pipe. Claudia toyed with her food and finally got up and shoved her plate back. She wandered about the kitchen for a few minutes and then went outside. Denny looked after her and put his fork down. Their mother's forehead carried a worried frown. Her glance traveled from the empty doorway to Denny's long face.

Claudia sat under the walnut tree in the back pasture most of the morning. Denny cleaned the stables without comment. Uncle Tom walked about muttering to himself. Denny stopped to listen. "Ought to go home and dig in my garden. Ought to be home, out of the way." Denny smiled to himself.

Uncle Tom had been waiting for them before breakfast. He looked up to see Denny watching him. "If I hadn't been so encouraging you might not even be in this mess."

"Uncle Tom," Denny said, "we couldn't do without you."

Finally he busied himself with the new stable. "If I was home I'd just worry about you," he told Denny. "Besides, I don't have enough to keep me busy. It's been great, coming over here every day." He stood for a moment. "I guess I'd better see about those boards from that old barn."

Denny stood watching him with his hands deep in his pockets. "What good will that do?" Denny muttered. "We'll probably be gone in thirty days."

"Sometimes work is good to keep you from thinking," Uncle Tom said. They both looked out across the pasture at Claudia. He handed Denny a hammer and a handful of nails. "We might as well use up all the short boards where they'll fit. Nail a board on that manger," he directed.

"Maybe you're right, Uncle Tom, but I feel as if this is the end of everything."

"Now, Denny," Uncle Tom put an arm across his shoul-

ders, "no matter how dark it is it has to get light sometime."

"That's easy to say," Denny retorted. "But it seems to
me that everything has been getting darker all along." He
struck a board hard with the hammer. "Just when is it
supposed to get better?"

"That's what we have to wait for," Uncle Tom said.
"But while we're waiting we'll go right on just as if
things were going to be all right."

"You sound like you're quoting from something,"
Denny said.

"Maybe I am," Uncle Tom said solemnly. "This isn't
new. People have always had trouble, and they've probably all found the way out, too."

"That sounds silly to me," Denny said finally, but he
thoughtfully fingered the nails and fitted the board to the
manger frame. The blows of his hammer were steady and
true and without anger. They were nearly finished when
Miss Butterfield and Miss Brown drove into the yard.

"We decided to ride early today." Alice Brown jumped
out of the car and slammed the door. Miss Butterfield
climbed out slowly, favoring her ankle, and limped over to
Uncle Tom. He stopped working and watched her walk.

"Do you think you should ride with that ankle as weak
as it is?" he asked.

"Oh, it's much better," Miss Butterfield said. "I'm just
not putting too much weight on it." She smiled sheepishly.
"It's not bad enough to keep me from riding. Besides,
we're just going to walk the horses along the lanes."

"How is Silver Wings this morning?" Alice Brown
peeked into the stable.

"Oh, she's fine," Uncle Tom told her. "The scratch is clean and healing." Denny busied himself picking up scraps of lumber and piling them carefully on the fireplace woodpile. The two women went to get their horses and Denny walked over and leaned against the framework of the new stall.

"I don't want to tell them about the ranch yet," he said.

"Time enough after your mother and father have signed the bill of sale," Uncle Tom said quietly.

"But we'll have to give them time to find another stable." Denny was grim. He ran a hand along the framework of the stall and looked about him, taking in the attractive ranch house and the matching stable.

"Let's take the pickup truck and go get those boards," Uncle Tom changed the subject, putting his tools away. Claudia climbed the pasture fence and trudged over to stand and watch the ladies saddle their horses.

"I wish you could go with us," Miss Butterfield said. "But I guess Cricket's leg is still quite sore."

"It's much better," Claudia replied. "When I walk her the swelling goes down and she hardly limps at all." She hesitated. "She has to get well soon."

"Well, I should think so," Alice Brown retorted. "It's no fun just walking a horse."

"I didn't mean that," Claudia spoke up.

"What did you mean, dear?" Miss Butterfield smiled down at her.

"Well, you see . . ." Claudia began. Then she was quiet. She studied the ground, twisting her hands, twining and untwining her fingers. "Nothing, nothing, I guess." She turned and ran into the house.

"Now, what's happened to her?" Alice Brown looked after her and then resumed bridling Silver Wings. Uncle Tom motioned to Denny and ambled up the back steps. Denny tossed the hammer aside and followed. Claudia stood looking out of the kitchen window, slowly sipping a glass of milk.

"You didn't tell Miss Butterfield about the ranch?" Uncle Tom began.

"No," Claudia said. "I was going to but I just couldn't."

"Uncle Tom says to wait until Mom and Dad sign the bill of sale," Denny told her.

"We should be hearing from Mr. Davis." Their mother filled a dish with chocolate-chip cookies and set them on the table. Then she poured Uncle Tom a cup of coffee.

"Why don't you call him?" Uncle Tom suggested.

"No, don't call, Mom," Claudia begged. "I don't even want to know."

"I'd just as soon get it over with," Denny said grimly. "We might as well find out now." He regarded Claudia for a moment. "We'll have to make new plans anyhow." Their mother hesitated and then picked up the telephone and dialed. Claudia set the glass of milk on the table and folded her hands tight across her chest.

"Mr. Davis," their mother spoke into the telephone, "I was wondering about the young man you brought out. Is it a sale?" Her glance flicked to each face intently watching her. "Oh, I see. Well, isn't there some way to work it out? I see. That's too bad."

"What's too bad?" Claudia wanted to know.

"The young man couldn't raise enough money," their mother explained.

"Then the ranch isn't sold?" Denny cried.

"No," their mother said. "We're right back where we started."

"Then we don't have to move!" Claudia smiled broadly. "Denny, we don't have to move."

"I'm getting dizzy," Denny laughed. "First we do, then we don't." He stuffed a cookie into his mouth and stood up. "Let's go get those boards so we can finish the stable." He stood waiting for Uncle Tom to finish the rest of his coffee. "You were right, Uncle Tom, we'll go right on working."

"The ranch is still up for sale," their mother reminded them. "Mr. Davis will probably find someone else."

"But, Mom, we have two boarders now," Denny said. "We're getting some lumber to finish the stables so we won't have to spend any money." His eyes probed hers. "Isn't everything all right now?"

"Perhaps, if we were up to date." His mother sighed. "But for the last two months we have just been keeping up the interest." She brushed a weary hand across her forehead. "We're two payments behind. If we had enough money to pick up those two payments we might be able to go on."

"Do you really mean that if we get the money for the payments we could stay on the ranch?" Claudia spoke quickly.

"Yes, if we keep the boarders we have now," her mother admitted. "Of course, your father would have to

177

approve. But I don't know where we are going to get the money to make up the payments." Claudia chewed on her lower lip thoughtfully. Denny stared across at her, but she avoided his eyes.

Claudia walked slowly to her room and came back with Cricket's pedigree papers. She stood holding them for a long time until her mother looked up at her. Then she held them out.

Her mother took the papers and sat looking at them. Denny moved his chair closer. Uncle Tom stepped up and looked over her shoulder.

"Revel's Duchess!" Denny whispered. "That even sounds like a lot of money."

"If you'll sign them, Mom, I'll take Cricket to Mr. Pomeroy." Claudia sighed, sat down, and leaned her chin in her hand.

"That will fix everything," Denny said brightly. "I knew right along that Claudia ought to sell Cricket. Now, you see, it is the best thing to do."

"Yes, you can say that." Claudia's lips trembled. "It isn't your horse."

"You know I wouldn't agree to this if it wasn't necessary," her mother said evenly.

"I hate to see her go, too," Uncle Tom said. "But it looks like it's the last resort. Naturally, you want to keep the ranch."

"I guess," Denny said quietly, "I guess if it came right down to it, I'd give up Blaze to keep the ranch."

"If we didn't have a horse I wouldn't care if we didn't keep the ranch," Claudia said stubbornly.

"Then why are we trying so hard?" Denny growled at her.

"So we can have the ranch and the horses," Claudia said heatedly.

"But we'll have one horse," Denny argued.

"Now, kids," Uncle Tom interrupted, "I know what's with you two." He grinned at their mother. "They know what they want, I'll say that." He became serious. "You children have discovered a way of life that you like, and you're fighting to keep it."

"Well, is that wrong?" Denny wanted to know.

"Of course not," Uncle Tom assured him. "But you have to remember that when you gain, you have to give away something. It isn't smooth sailing ever. But every time you sacrifice you gain a little more."

"You don't make sense, Uncle Tom." Claudia was frank.

"I guess I don't," Uncle Tom admitted.

"Uncle Tom means that trouble makes better people out of us," their mother explained. "Finding your way out of trouble builds character."

"Well, we're certainly a couple of characters then," Denny retorted grimly.

"You mean we have to go through things like this all the time?" Claudia was incredulous.

"It isn't all children who have an opportunity to help their parents as you have," Uncle Tom explained.

"Gosh, do people have trouble like this all the time?" Claudia's eyes were wide with wonder.

"Well, no," their mother hastened to say. "We've just been through a trying period but I think we'll work it out." She smiled at them. "When we do we shall all be happy for a long, long time."

"But maybe if we hadn't wanted a ranch and horses we wouldn't have had so much trouble," Claudia said. "Is it wrong to want them?"

"Of course not," their mother said. "As long as you're willing to make the sacrifices it takes to get them."

"And I have to give Cricket up," Claudia said at last.

"It isn't as though you'd never see her again," Denny hastened to say. "You could go see her every week, if you wanted to."

"I guess so," Claudia said finally. "Well, if you'll sign the papers, Mom, I'll take her to Mr. Pomeroy."

"Tell you what let's do," Uncle Tom began. "Denny and I'll go get those boards we were talking about and then we'll bring the horse trailer back and deliver Cricket."

"I suppose that is the best thing to do," their mother said. Claudia was quiet. She stood holding the papers close in her arms. Denny followed Uncle Tom out the back door.

It took them two hours to pull the boards off the building and load them. Then they drove back to the yard and began to pile them beside the new stall. They finished and Denny put up the tail gate of the trailer. His mother came out to meet them.

"Gee, Mom, we thought for a while we weren't going to get those boards." Denny laughed. "The guy wanted us to tear down the whole barn." He looked around. "Where's Claudia? I thought she'd be waiting."

"She isn't that anxious," Uncle Tom said. "She's

probably down by the walnut tree. Better call her so we can go.''

Denny jumped the fence and started across the pasture. Uncle Tom and their mother walked to the fence and watched him. Denny stopped and turned back.

''She isn't over there,'' he called. Denny shaded his forehead with his hand. He scanned the whole area. ''Cricket isn't out here, either.''

''She surely didn't go for a ride,'' his mother said anxiously. ''Not with Cricket's leg the way it is.''

''Well, she isn't out here,'' Denny finally announced. Uncle Tom hurried to look in the stable but returned shaking his head.

''She must have gone for a ride,'' his mother insisted.

''No,'' Uncle Tom said grimly. ''She wouldn't ride Cricket, knowing her leg isn't well.'' He was thoughtful. ''No, it's something else.''

Claudia pulled Cricket to a stop. She slipped a hand along Cricket's smooth neck. ''Are you tired, Cricket?'' she said softly. Cricket nickered low and nudged her with her muzzle. Claudia sat down on the culvert and Cricket began to nibble at the roadside grass. ''We'll rest a while.'' She looked up the road. ''We've still a long way to go. But I'll have all this time to spend with you. Of course, I'll come out to see you often but it won't ever be like this again.'' She sighed. ''Right this minute you still belong to me.'' They rested.

Finally Claudia led the little mare along the shoulder of the road. Once she stopped and looked back but the road was empty. They trudged on.

"When did you see Claudia last?" Uncle Tom asked as he backed the trailer and prepared to turn the pickup truck around.

"Why, when . . ." Their mother was thoughtful. "Why, when you and Denny left to get the lumber."

"That means she has two hours' start." Uncle Tom gripped the wheel. His eyes were narrowed with worry and his mouth set in a tight line. He waited for Denny and his mother to get in and then wheeled the pickup truck and trailer down the driveway. He slowed and came to a stop as they reached the entrance to the ranch.

"If she's walking it would take her quite a while to get to Mr. Pomeroy's," Denny suggested. Uncle Tom looked up and down the road and then paused as a Western Union boy stopped and read the sign at the gate.

"Mrs. Wolff?" He walked up to the side of the pickup truck.

"I'm Mrs. Wolff." Denny's mother glanced at Uncle Tom and Denny. The boy handed her a telegram. She signed for it. "I hope nothing has happened to Jim."

"Open it, Mom," Denny urged. He watched her face as she read the few lines on the yellow sheet. Her mouth began to quirk at the corners and then she flung her arm around Denny's shoulder. Denny took the telegram and read it aloud. "Got promotion. Take ranch off market!"

"Well, that's fine!" Uncle Tom smiled and nodded. "I sure didn't like the thought of you folks giving up this place."

"Hear that, Uncle Tom! We don't have to move," Denny cried. "Now, we have to hurry and find Claudia."

Uncle Tom put the pickup truck in gear and turned down the road.

"You'd better go slow," Denny's mother said. "We don't want to miss her."

"How can you miss a girl walking a horse?" Denny wanted to know but he leaned out the window and began to watch. They stopped at every crossroad and looked carefully around. "I hope she didn't take any short cuts. If she cut through an orchard we wouldn't be able to see her."

They neared the Pomeroy ranch. Alongside the road was a long line of pepper trees. It was Denny who saw her first. Claudia was sitting on the ground rubbing Cricket's leg with both hands. When Uncle Tom stopped the pickup truck she looked up and they could see the streaks down her cheeks where the tears had coursed through the dust. She didn't smile when she saw them but gave all her attention to rubbing Cricket's leg with long strokes.

"Claudia, Claudia, we don't have to sell the ranch!" The words tumbled from Denny's lips and he knelt beside her. "We just heard from Dad. He got his promotion!" He grinned. "He's a major!"

Claudia stopped rubbing Cricket's leg. She looked at Denny for a long time. She stared at Uncle Tom, clambered to her feet, and ran to her mother. "Is Denny right? Is he telling the truth?"

"Yes, dear." Her mother put an arm around her shoulders. "We just got a telegram from your father."

"Oh, Mom!" Claudia hid her face against her mother.

"You won't have to sell Cricket," her mother said.

"You mean you're not going to sell Cricket?" Denny went back on his heels.

"The ranch will mean more to Claudia if she has her own horse," his mother said. "We will still have to be very careful about the way we manage things but I think we can make it."

"But we have to make up two payments," Denny protested.

"We could use the money we saved for hay," Claudia said. "We can put it back when we get next month's

board money and what you make at Kendall's and the lawns you cut and my baby sitting.''

"That's going to be hard." Denny was thoughtful.

"With your Dad's raise in rank and more pay," Uncle Tom said, "you'll make it."

"Maybe we can get another boarder," Denny said hopefully.

"That remains to be seen," their mother said. "Let's be thankful with what we have."

"And Cricket is still mine." Claudia smiled and ran to the little mare and threw her arms around her neck. "Maybe I can raise a colt and sell it to Mr. Pomeroy." Claudia's eyes were bright. "He said he wanted a colt from Cricket."

"I'm sure you children will figure out some way to make everything work." Uncle Tom chuckled. He knelt beside Cricket. "Now let's see about this leg."

"Cricket started to limp again," Claudia said. "I thought if I didn't ride her she would be all right."

"She's probably just tired." Uncle Tom examined her leg and ran a practiced hand up and down, pressing with his fingers. "Too far to walk on a sore leg."

"Why didn't you wait?" Denny wanted to know. "You knew we were going to bring the trailer back."

"Yes, Claudia, why did you take Cricket without saying anything to me?" her mother put in.

"I just wanted to stay with Cricket as long as I could," Claudia told them. "It doesn't take very long to drive out to Mr. Pomeroy's with a trailer."

"Well, you gave us a scare," Denny said stiffly.

"Well, I just had to figure something out," Claudia
186

answered. She leaned against Cricket and smiled at them all. "It seems like all I do is figure something out."

"If it wasn't for you children and your figuring we could never keep the ranch." Their mother gave each an affectionate and proud glance. She took her handkerchief and wiped at the tear-stained dust that had dried on Claudia's face.

"But Dad's promotion . . ." Denny put in.

"Your Dad's promotion is important," their mother agreed, "but we still couldn't do without your help."

"Yep," Uncle Tom said, "you've proved what you can do." He chuckled. "Your Dad is going to be mighty surprised when he comes home on leave. Maybe, if your stable keeps growing, you'll let me build a room and I'll move over here. I almost live here now."

"You know," Denny was thoughtful, "I feel real good."

Claudia hugged Cricket again. "You see." She smiled at all of them. "Things really do turn out all right."

B 1